FRY GUYS

BATTER OF THE BANDS

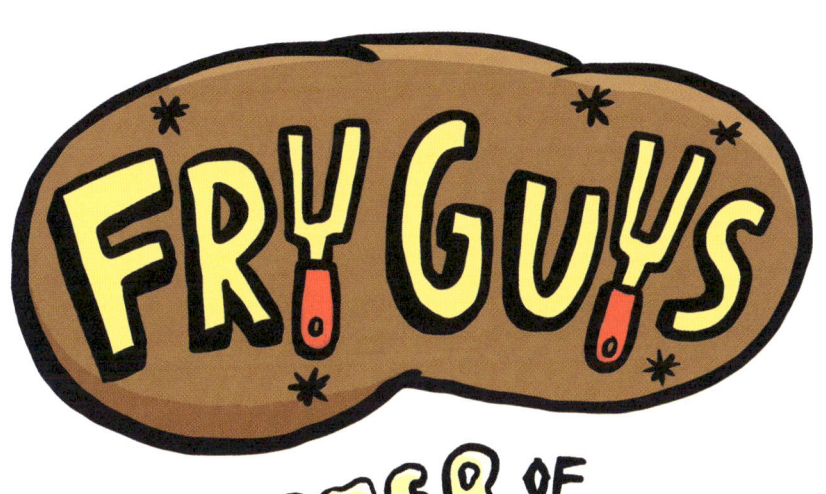

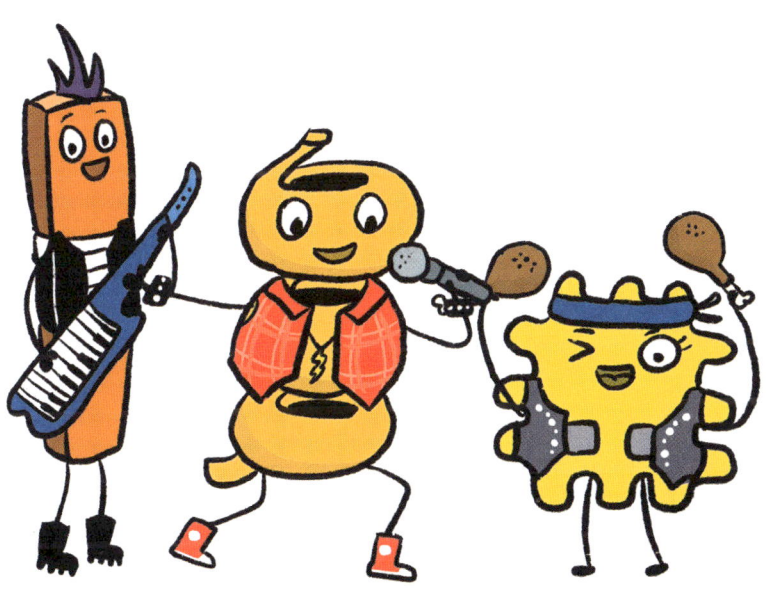

© 2024 Andrews McMeel Publishing. Written by Eric Geron. Illustrated by Jannie Ho. All rights reserved. Printed in China. No part of this book may be used or reproduced in any manner whatsoever without written permission except in the case of reprints in the context of reviews.

Andrews McMeel Publishing
a division of Andrews McMeel Universal
1130 Walnut Street, Kansas City, Missouri 64106

www.andrewsmcmeel.com

24 25 26 27 28 SDB 10 9 8 7 6 5 4 3 2 1

ISBN: 978-1-5248-7944-0

Library of Congress Control Number: 2024935014

Editor: Erinn Pascal
Art Director: Julie Barnes
Production Editor: David Shaw
Production Manager: Chuck Harper

Made by:
RR Donnelley (Guangdong) Printing Solutions Company Ltd
Address and location of manufacturer:
No. 2, Minzhu Road, Daning, Humen Town,
Dongguan City, Guangdong Province, China 523930
1st Printing — 6/17/24

ATTENTION: SCHOOLS AND BUSINESSES
Andrews McMeel books are available at quantity discounts with bulk purchase for educational, business, or sales promotional use. For information, please e-mail the Andrews McMeel Publishing Special Sales Department: sales@amuniversal.com.

FRY GUYS
BATTER OF THE BANDS

Eric Geron

Jannie Ho

Andrews McMeel
PUBLISHING®

CHAPTER 1 Spud-Rock

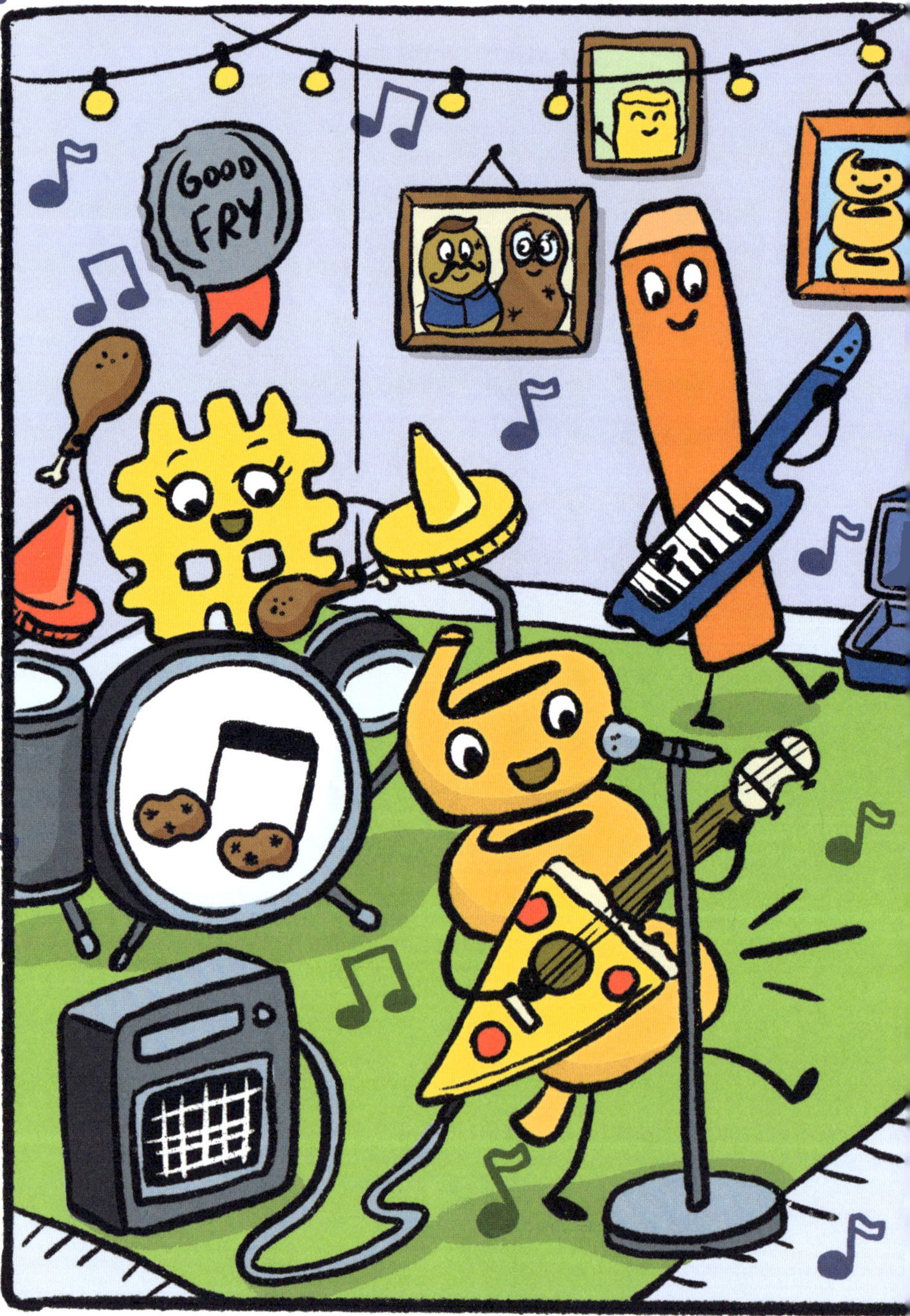
GOOD FRY

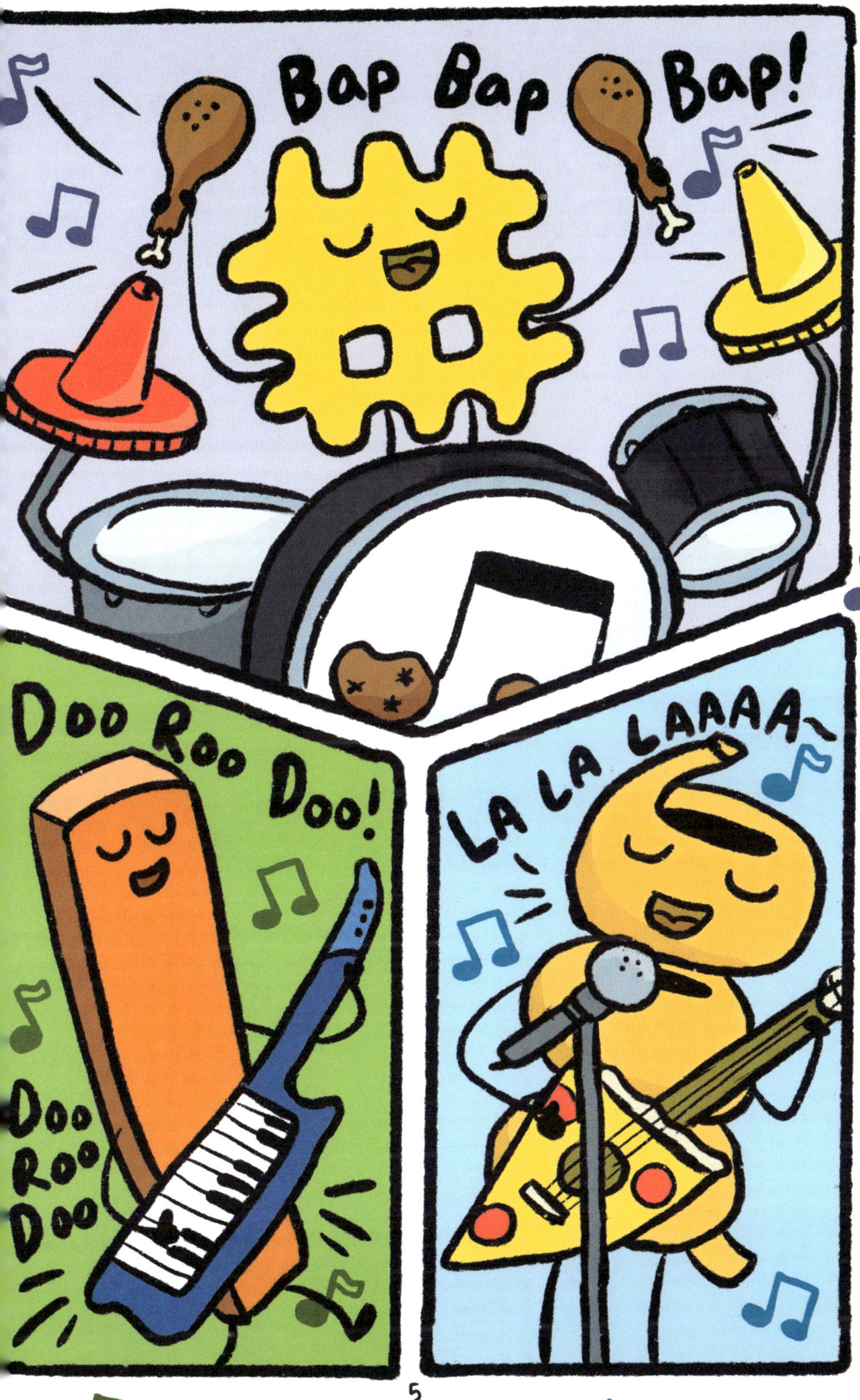
Bap Bap Bap!
DOO ROO DOO!
DOO ROO DOO
LA LA LAAAA~

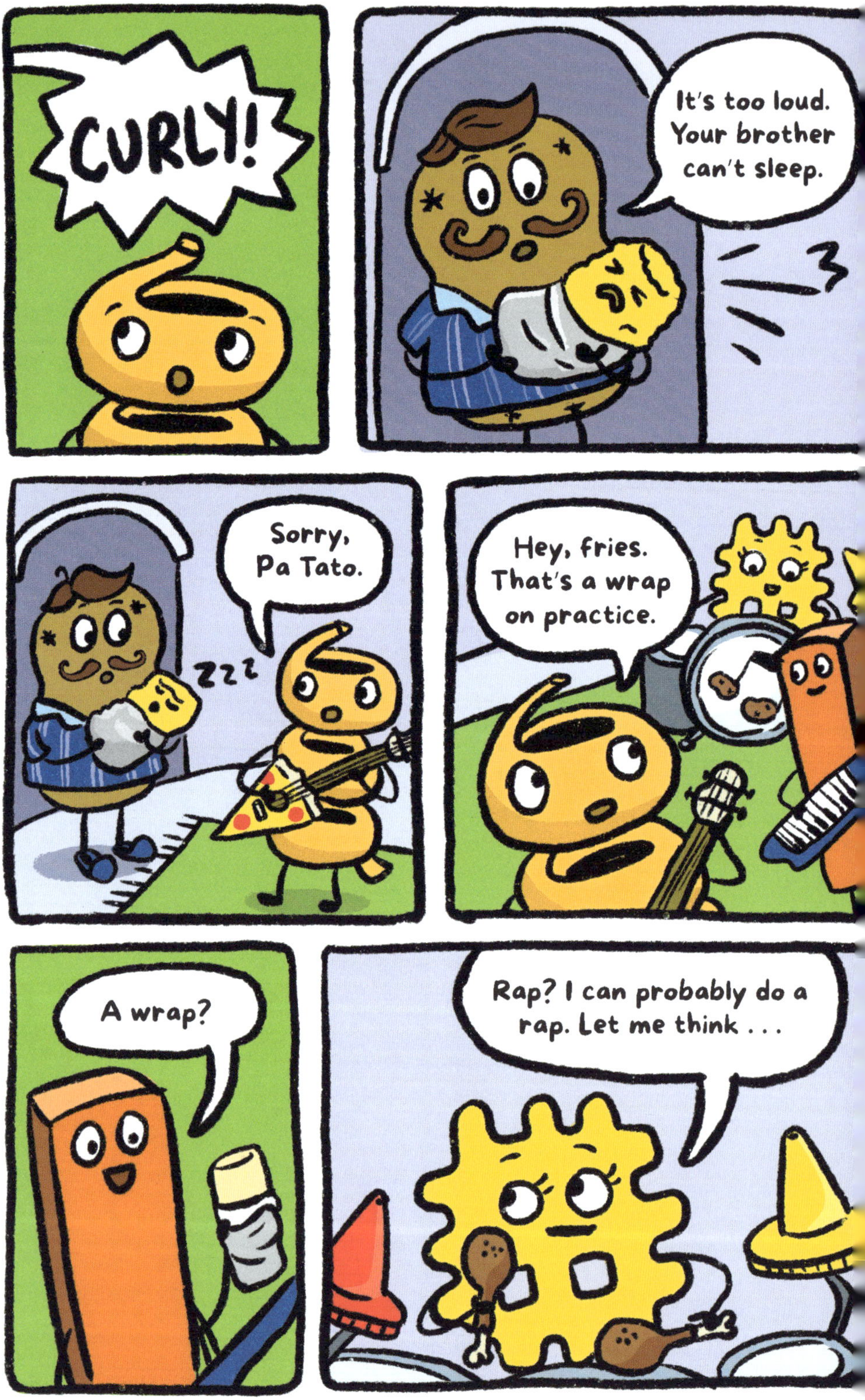
CURLY!
It's too loud. Your brother can't sleep.
Sorry, Pa Tato.
ZZZ
Hey, fries. That's a wrap on practice.
A wrap?
Rap? I can probably do a rap. Let me think . . .

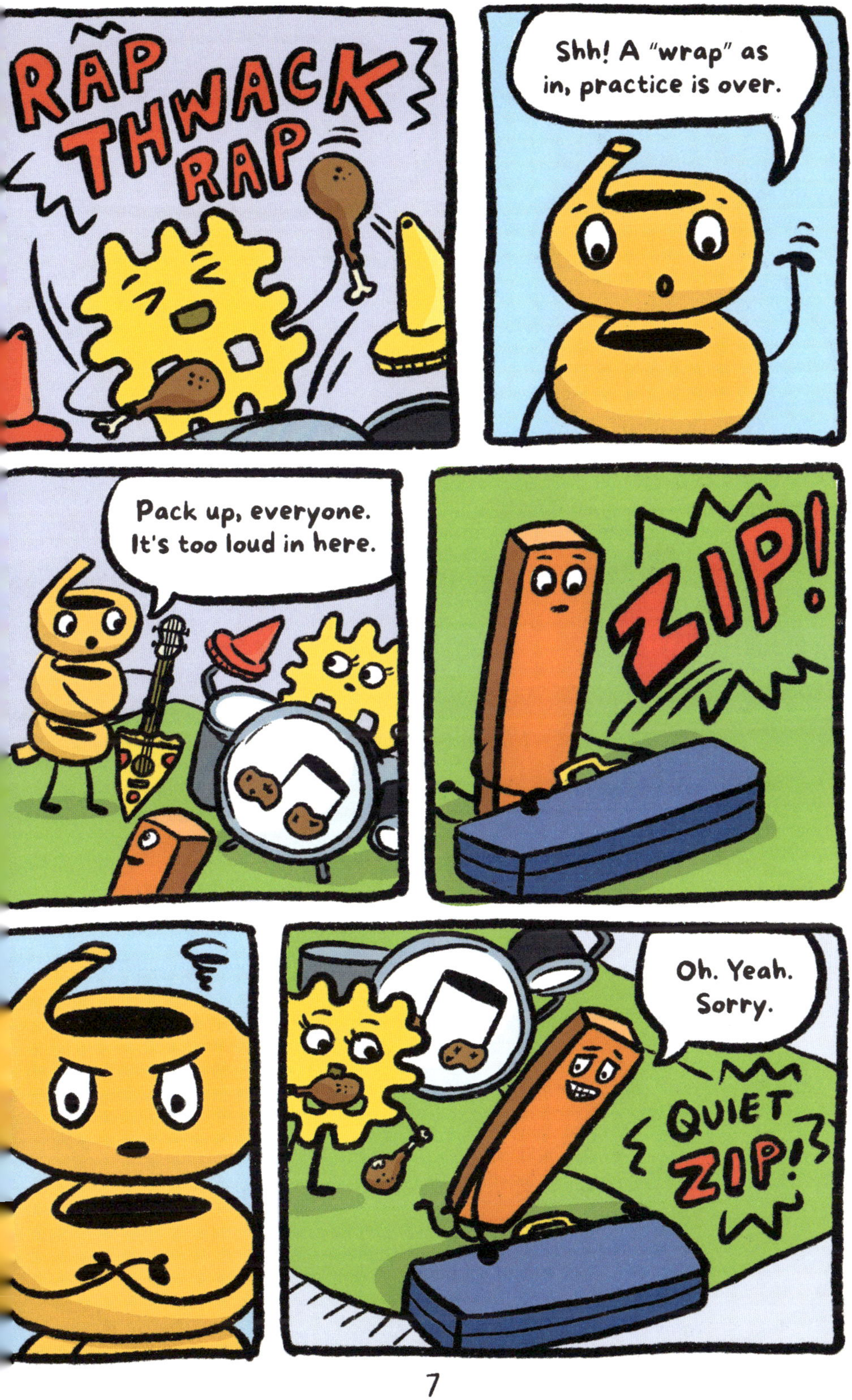
RAP
THWACK
RAP
Shh! A "wrap" as in, practice is over.
Pack up, everyone. It's too loud in here.
ZIP!
Oh. Yeah. Sorry.
QUIET ZIP!

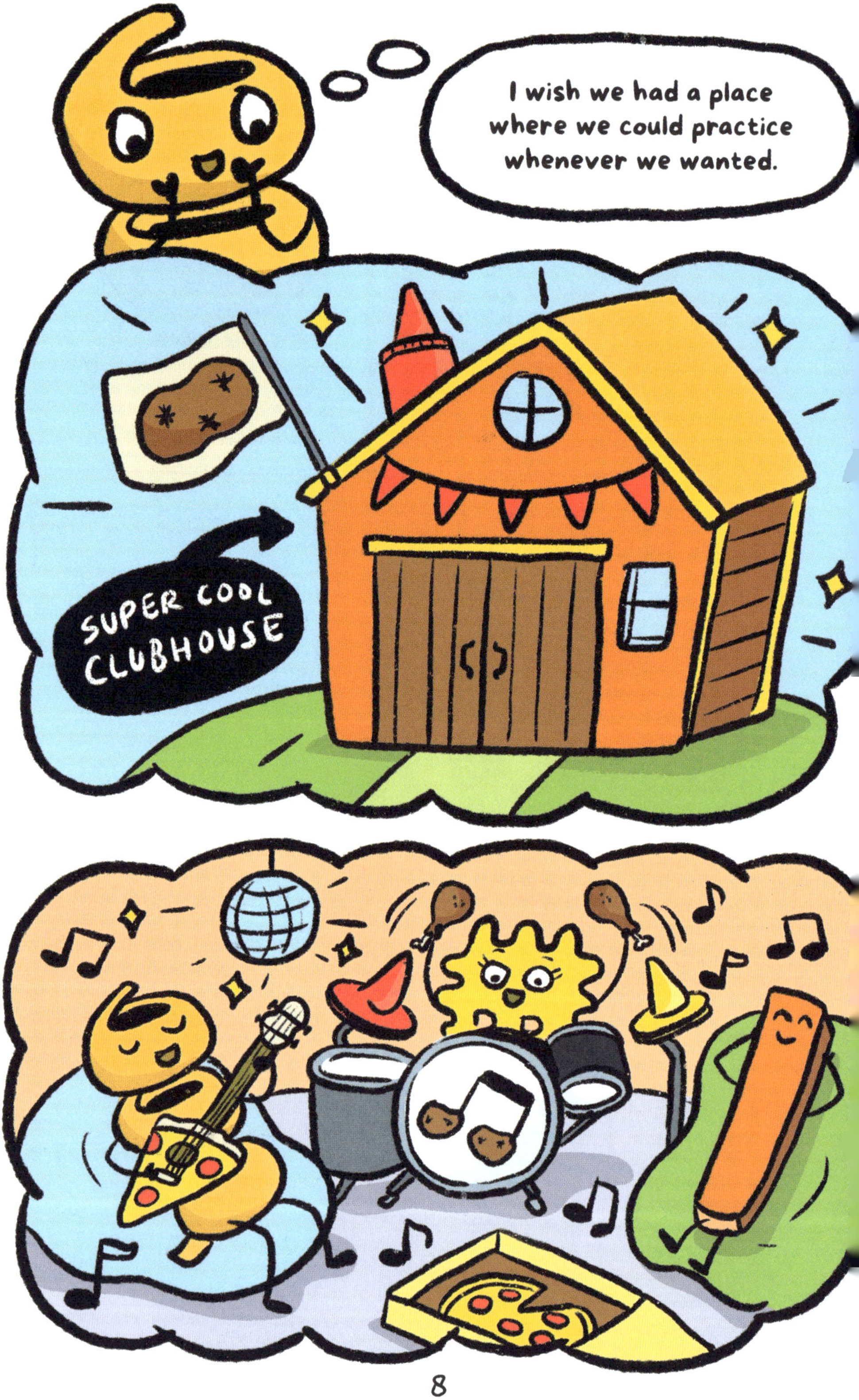
I wish we had a place where we could practice whenever we wanted.
SUPER COOL CLUBHOUSE

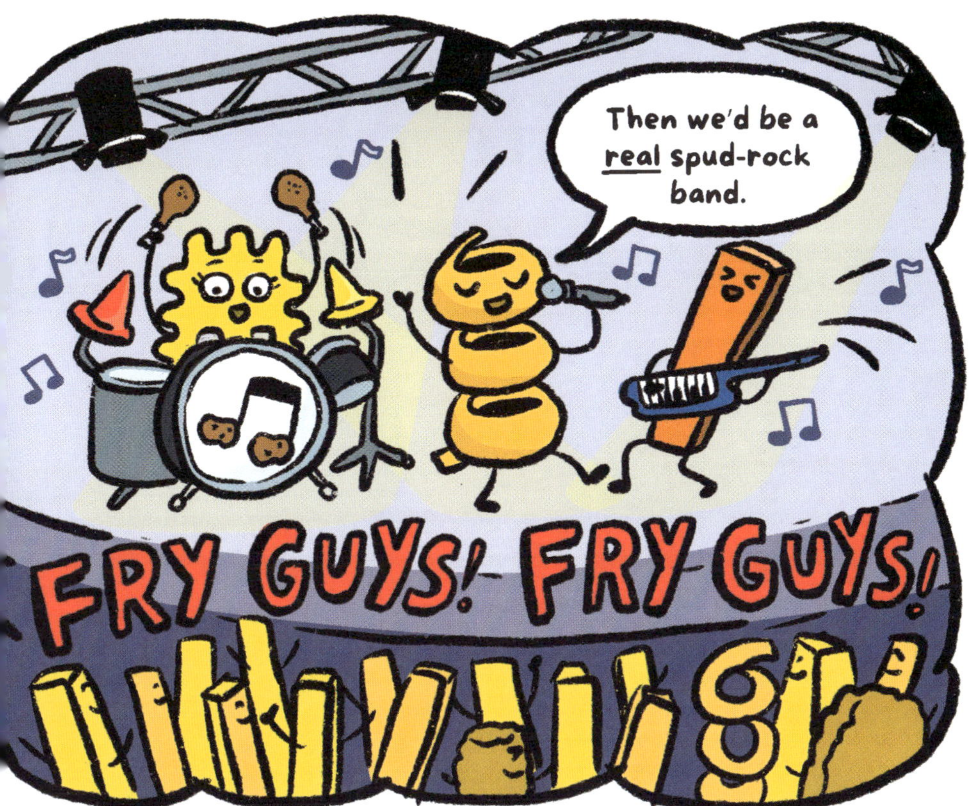
Then we'd be a real spud-rock band.
FRY GUYS! FRY GUYS!

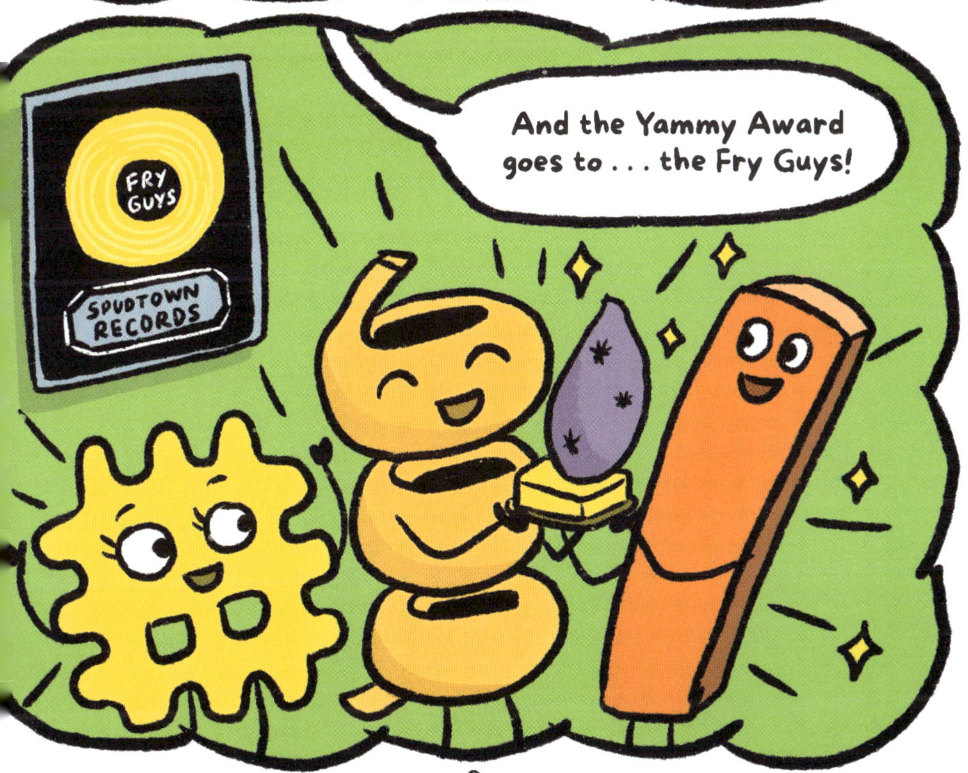
And the Yammy Award goes to . . . the Fry Guys!
FRY GUYS
SPUDTOWN RECORDS

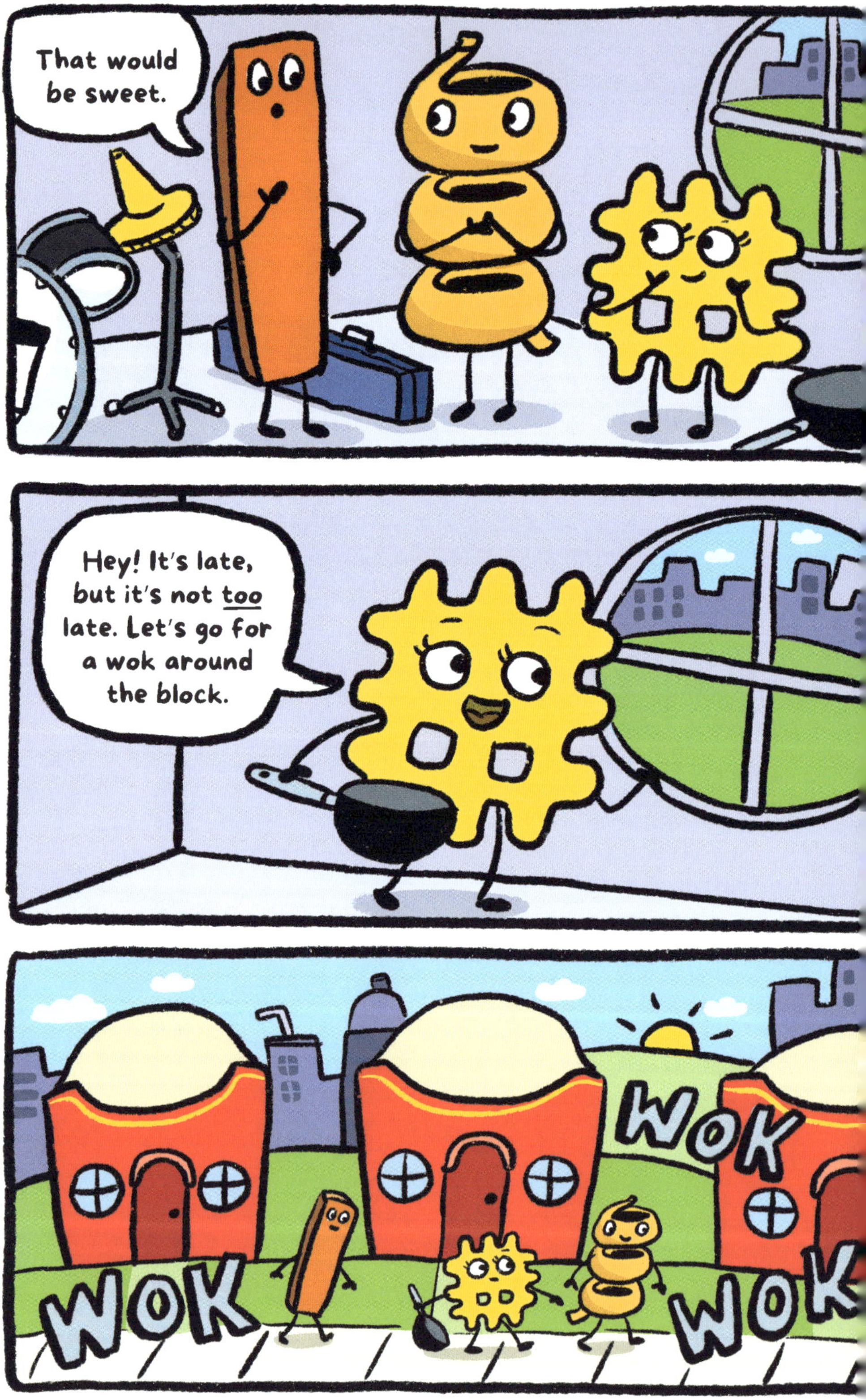
That would be sweet.
Hey! It's late, but it's not too late. Let's go for a wok around the block.
WOK
WOK
WOK

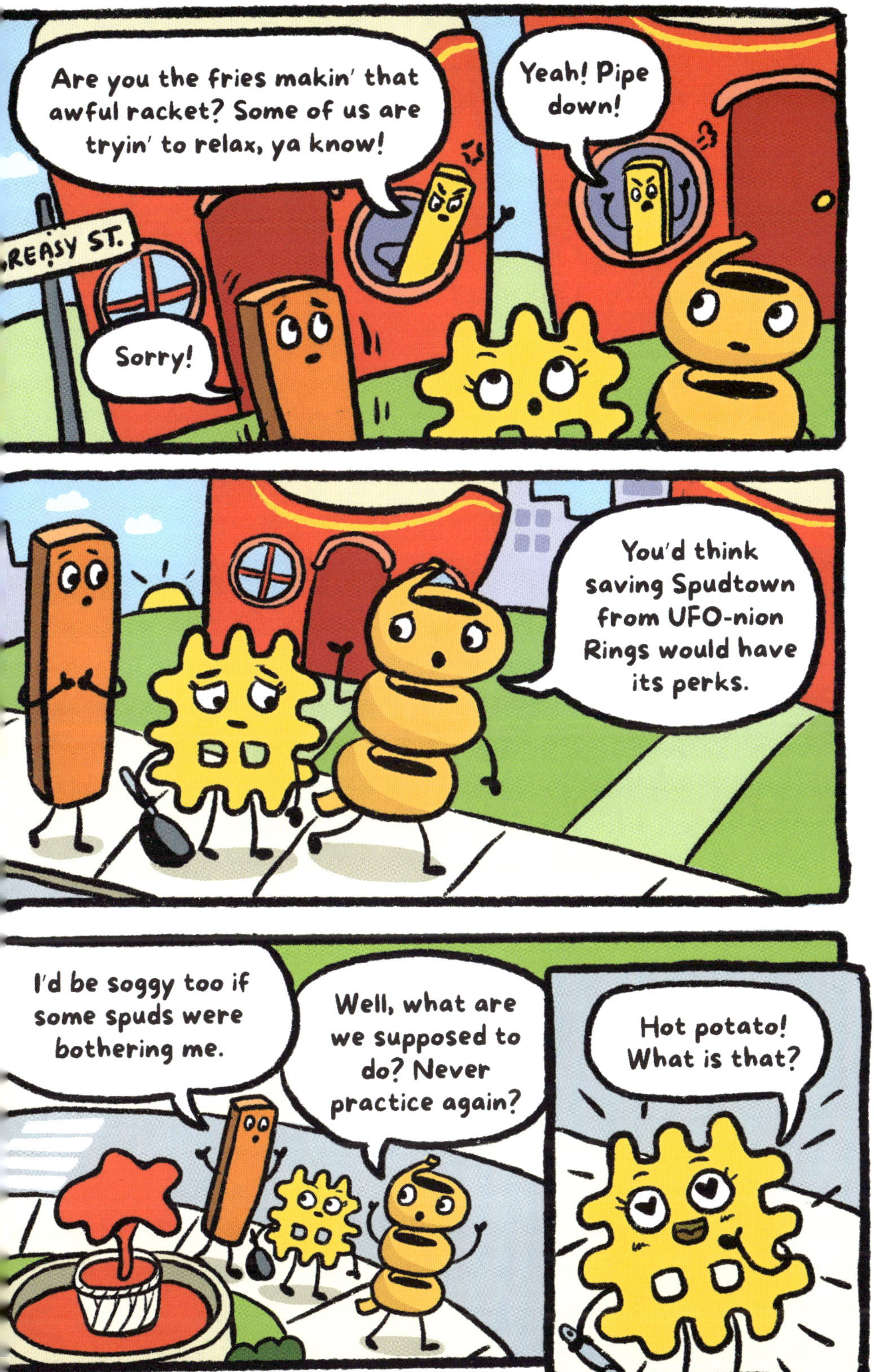
Are you the fries makin' that awful racket? Some of us are tryin' to relax, ya know!
Yeah! Pipe down!
REASY ST.
Sorry!
You'd think saving Spudtown from UFO-nion Rings would have its perks.
I'd be soggy too if some spuds were bothering me.
Well, what are we supposed to do? Never practice again?
Hot potato! What is that?

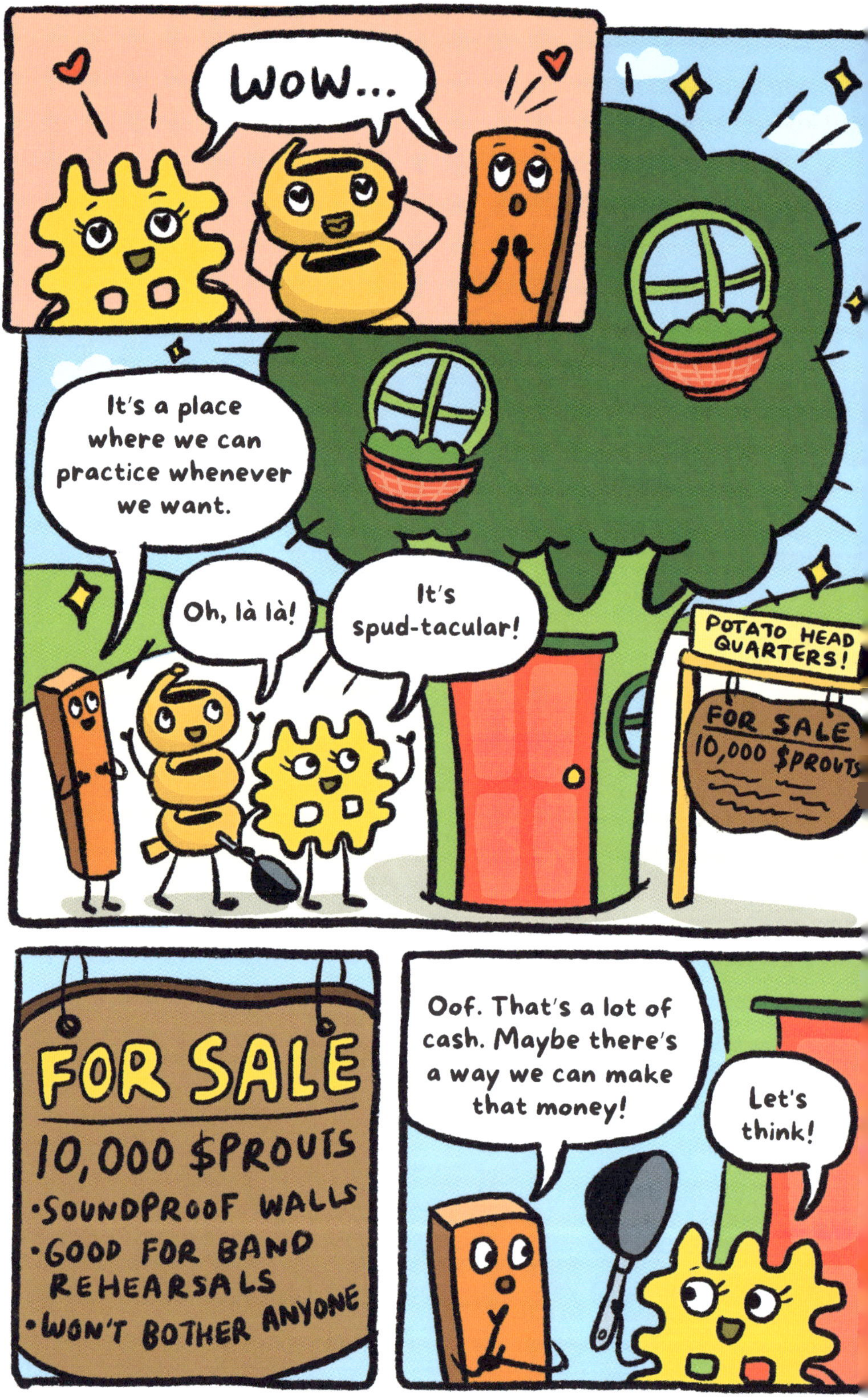
WOW...
It's a place where we can practice whenever we want.
Oh, là là!
It's spud-tacular!
POTATO HEAD QUARTERS!
FOR SALE 10,000 $PROUTS
FOR SALE
10,000 $PROUTS
•SOUNDPROOF WALLS
•GOOD FOR BAND REHEARSALS
•WON'T BOTHER ANYONE
Oof. That's a lot of cash. Maybe there's a way we can make that money!
Let's think!

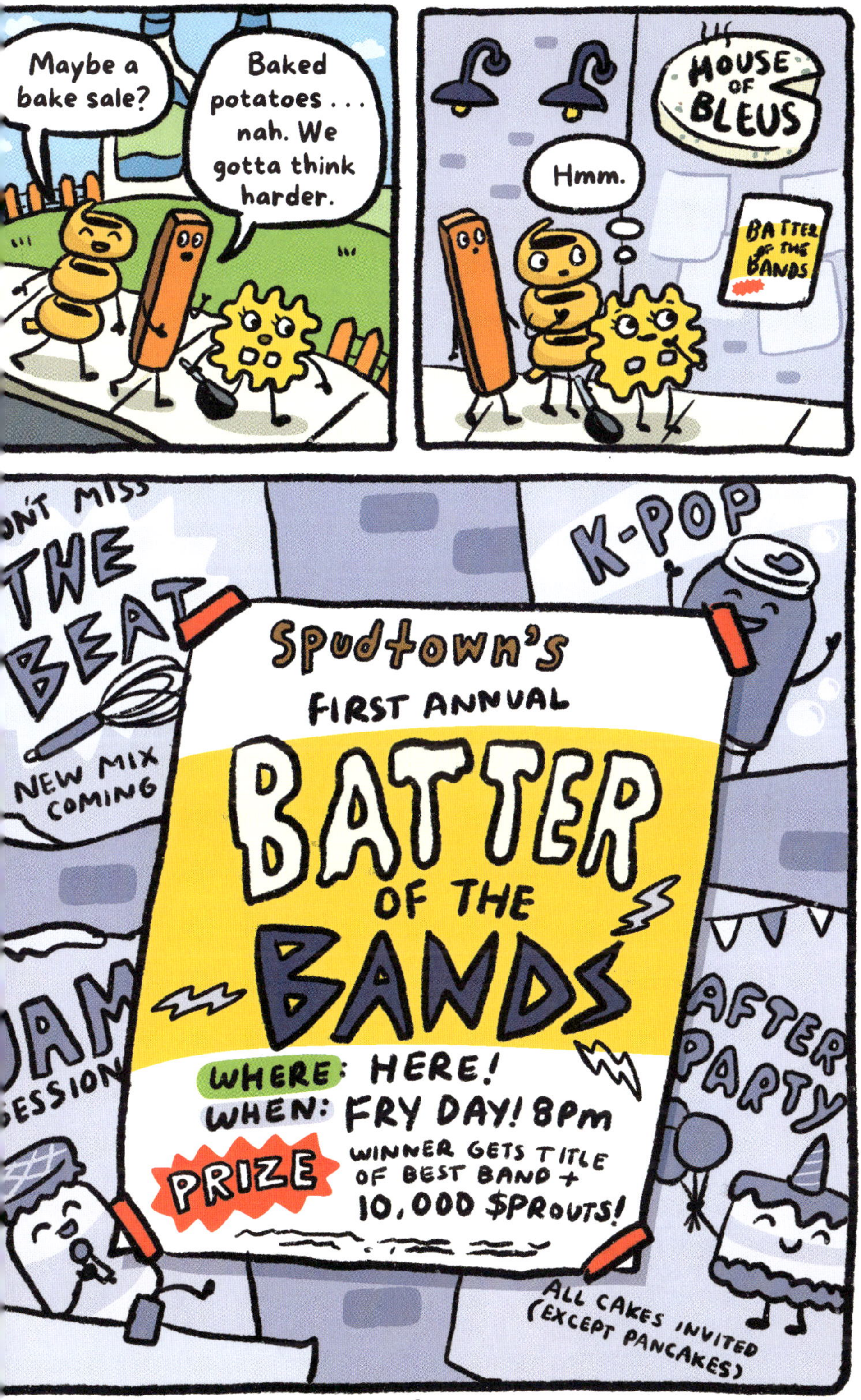
Maybe a bake sale?
Baked potatoes . . . nah. We gotta think harder.
HOUSE OF BLEUS
Hmm.
BATTER OF THE BANDS
DON'T MISS THE BEAT
NEW MIX COMING
K-POP
SPUDTOWN'S FIRST ANNUAL
BATTER OF THE BANDS
WHERE: HERE!
WHEN: FRY DAY! 8PM
PRIZE
WINNER GETS TITLE OF BEST BAND + 10,000 $PROUTS!
JAM SESSION
AFTER PARTY
ALL CAKES INVITED (EXCEPT PANCAKES)

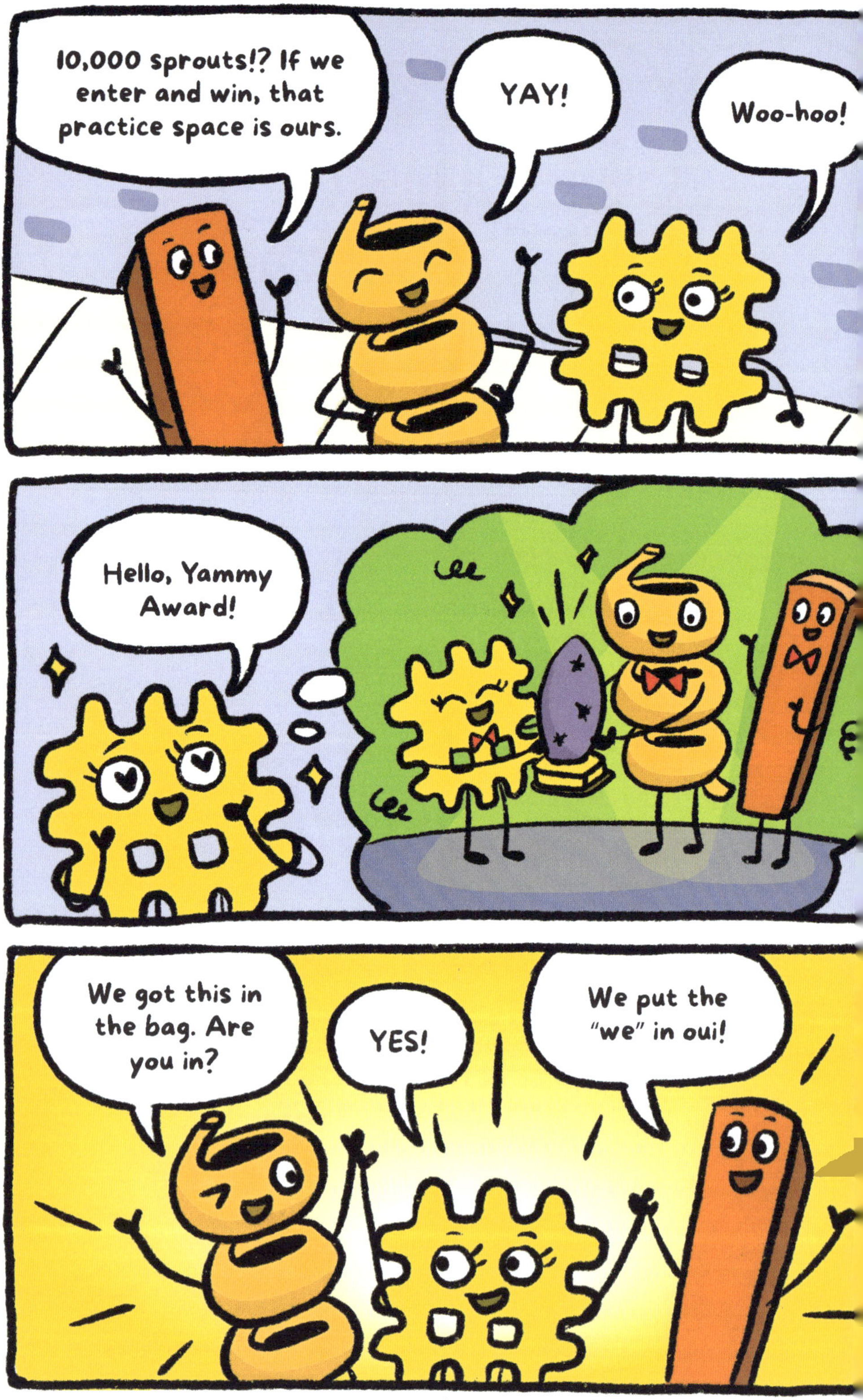
10,000 sprouts!? If we enter and win, that practice space is ours.
YAY!
Woo-hoo!
Hello, Yammy Award!
We got this in the bag. Are you in?
YES!
We put the "we" in oui!

CHAPTER 2 House of Bleus

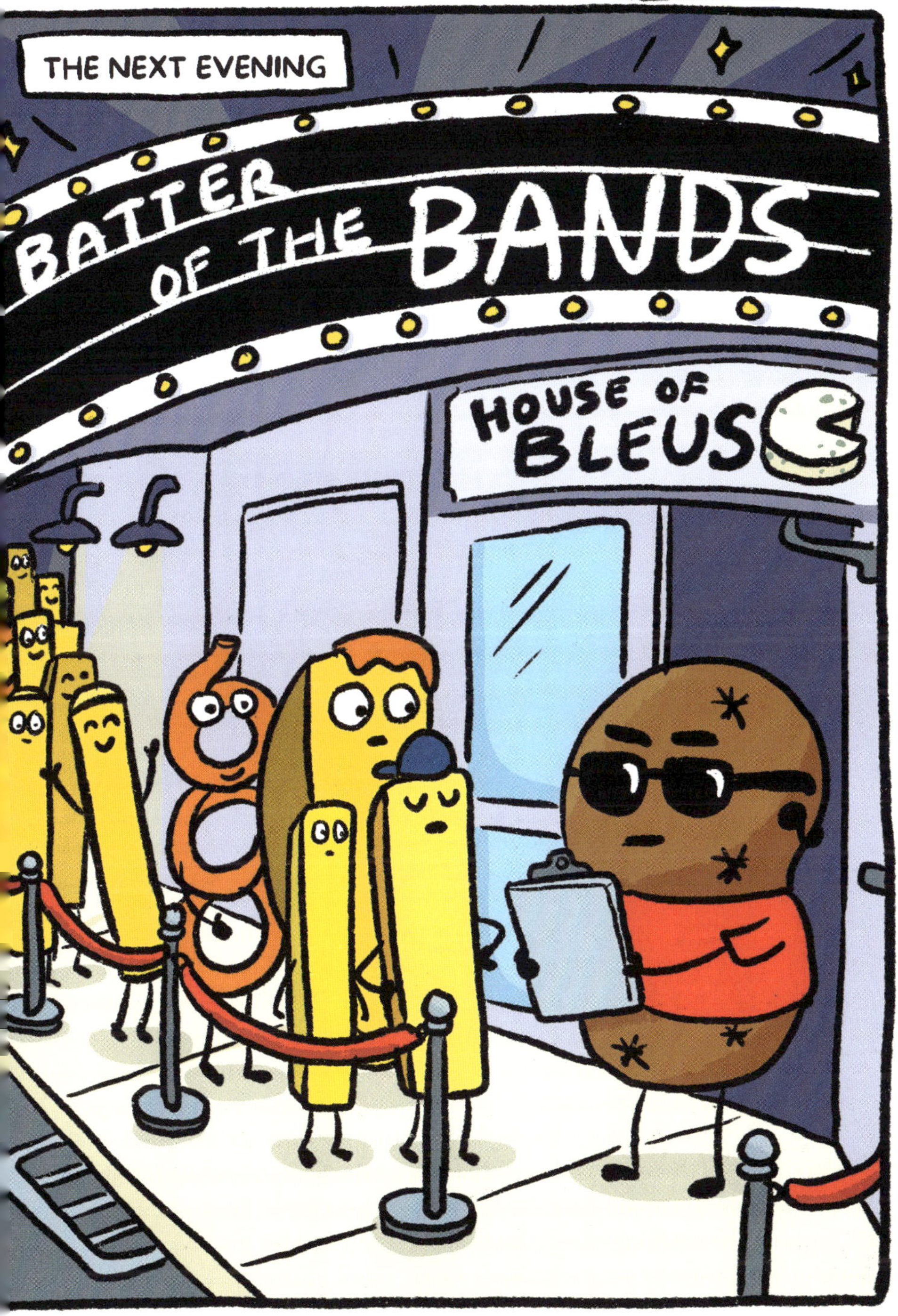
THE NEXT EVENING
BATTER OF THE BANDS
HOUSE OF BLEUS

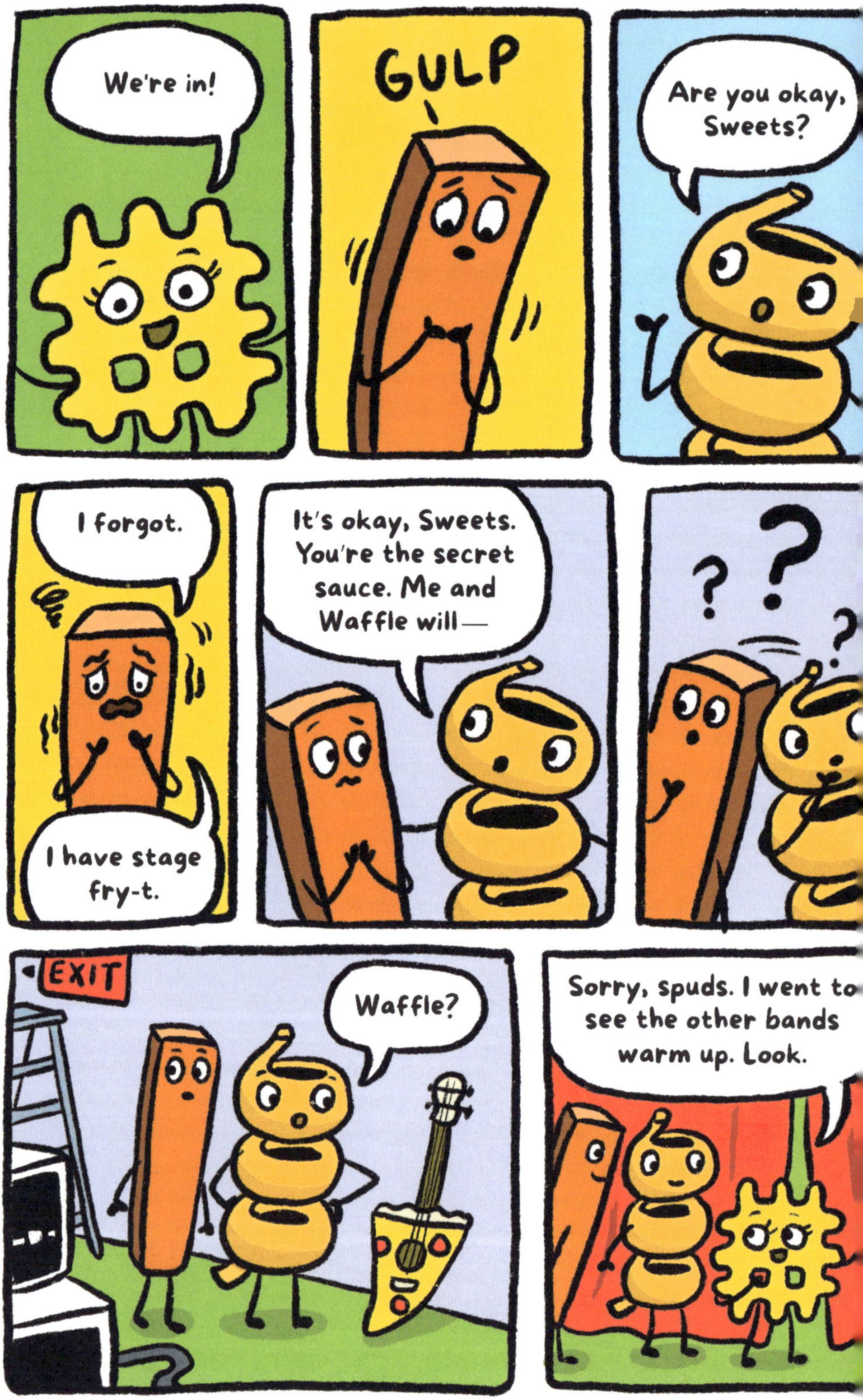
We're in!
GULP
Are you okay, Sweets?
I forgot.
I have stage fry-t.
It's okay, Sweets. You're the secret sauce. Me and Waffle will—
? ? ?
EXIT
Waffle?
Sorry, spuds. I went to see the other bands warm up. Look.

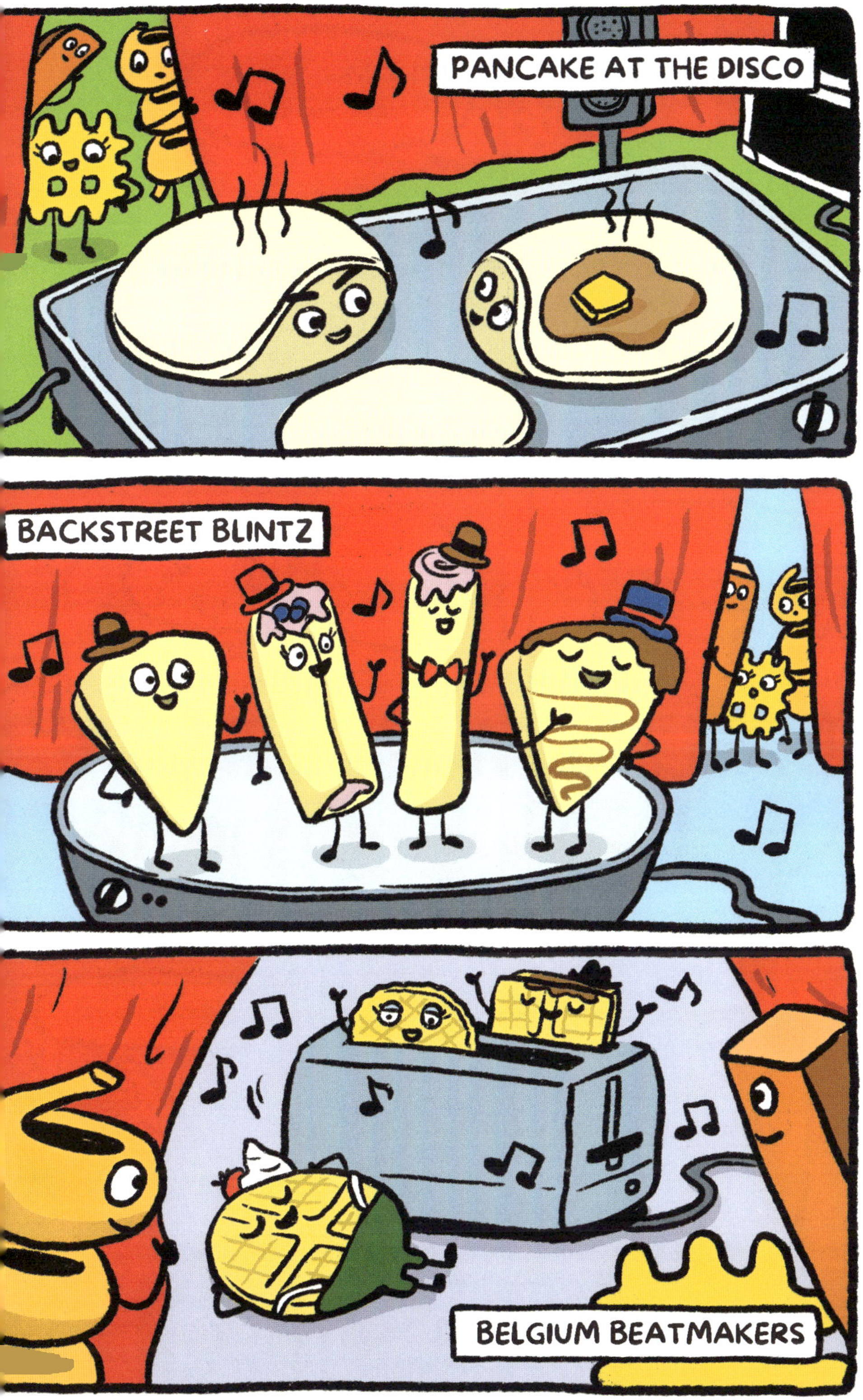
PANCAKE AT THE DISCO
BACKSTREET BLINTZ
BELGIUM BEATMAKERS

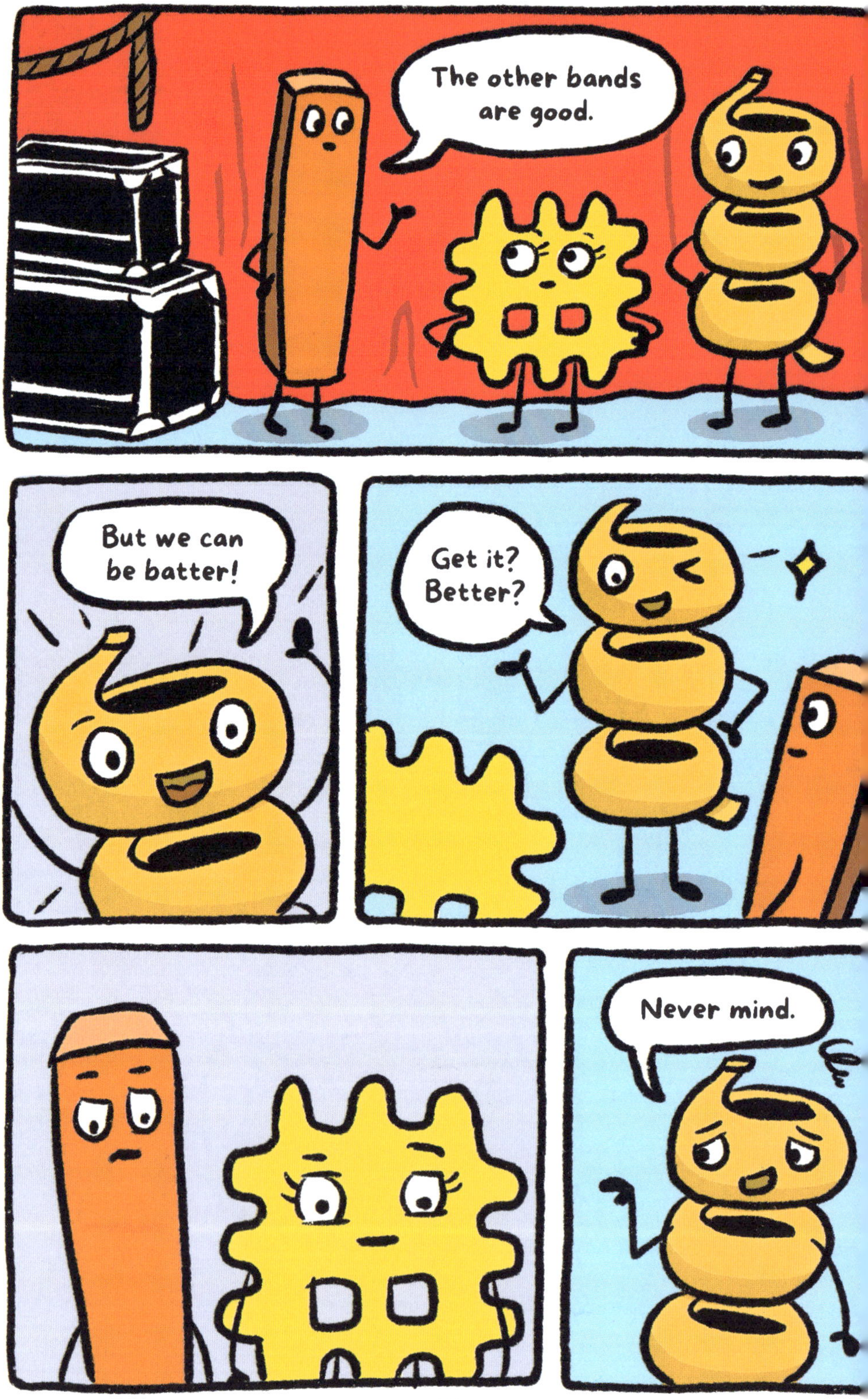
The other bands are good.
But we can be batter!
Get it? Better?
Never mind.

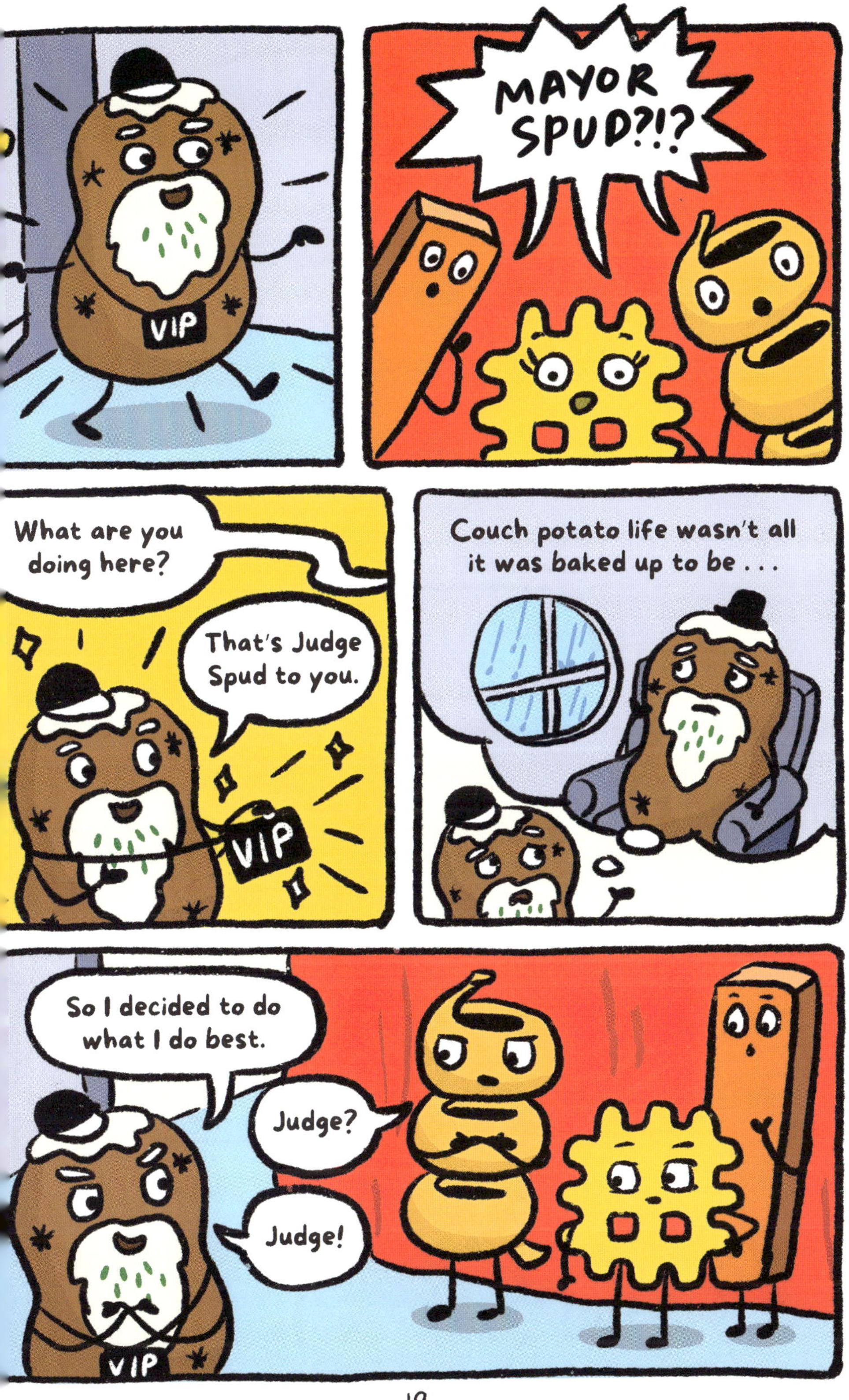
MAYOR SPUD?!?
What are you doing here?
That's Judge Spud to you.
VIP
Couch potato life wasn't all it was baked up to be . . .
So I decided to do what I do best.
Judge?
Judge!
VIP

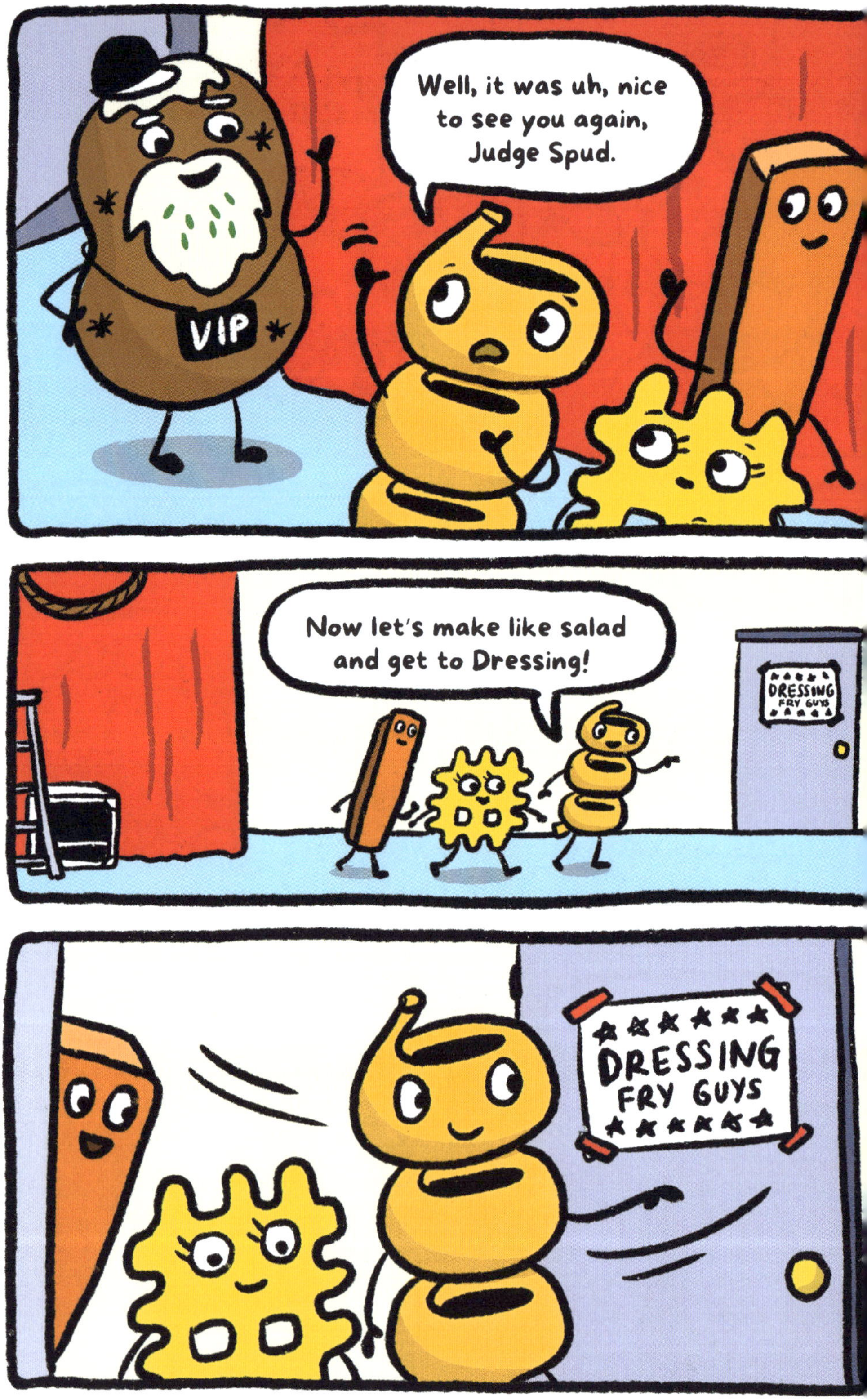
Well, it was uh, nice to see you again, Judge Spud.
VIP
Now let's make like salad and get to Dressing!
DRESSING
FRY GUYS
DRESSING
FRY GUYS

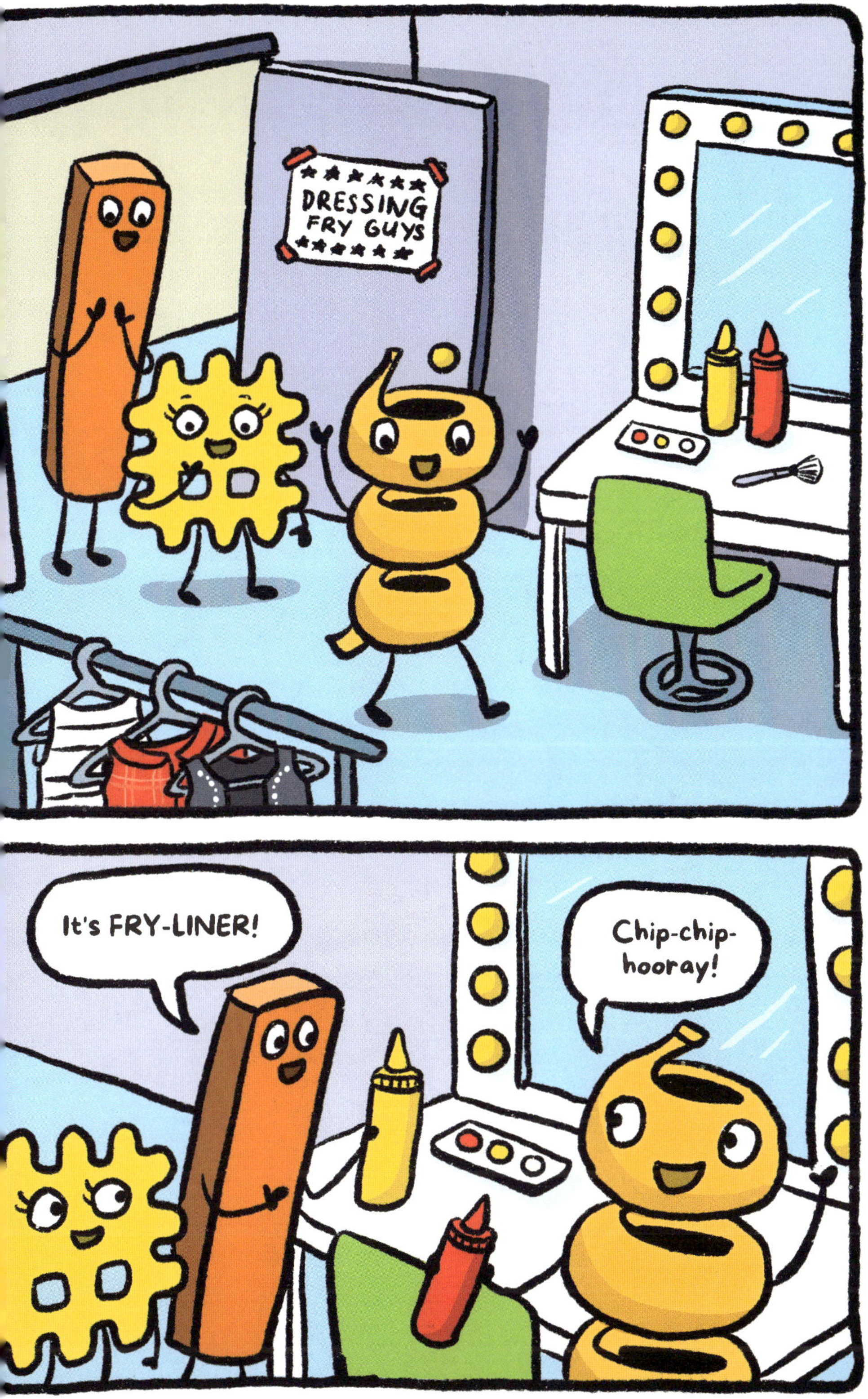
DRESSING
FRY GUYS
It's FRY-LINER!
Chip-chip-
hooray!

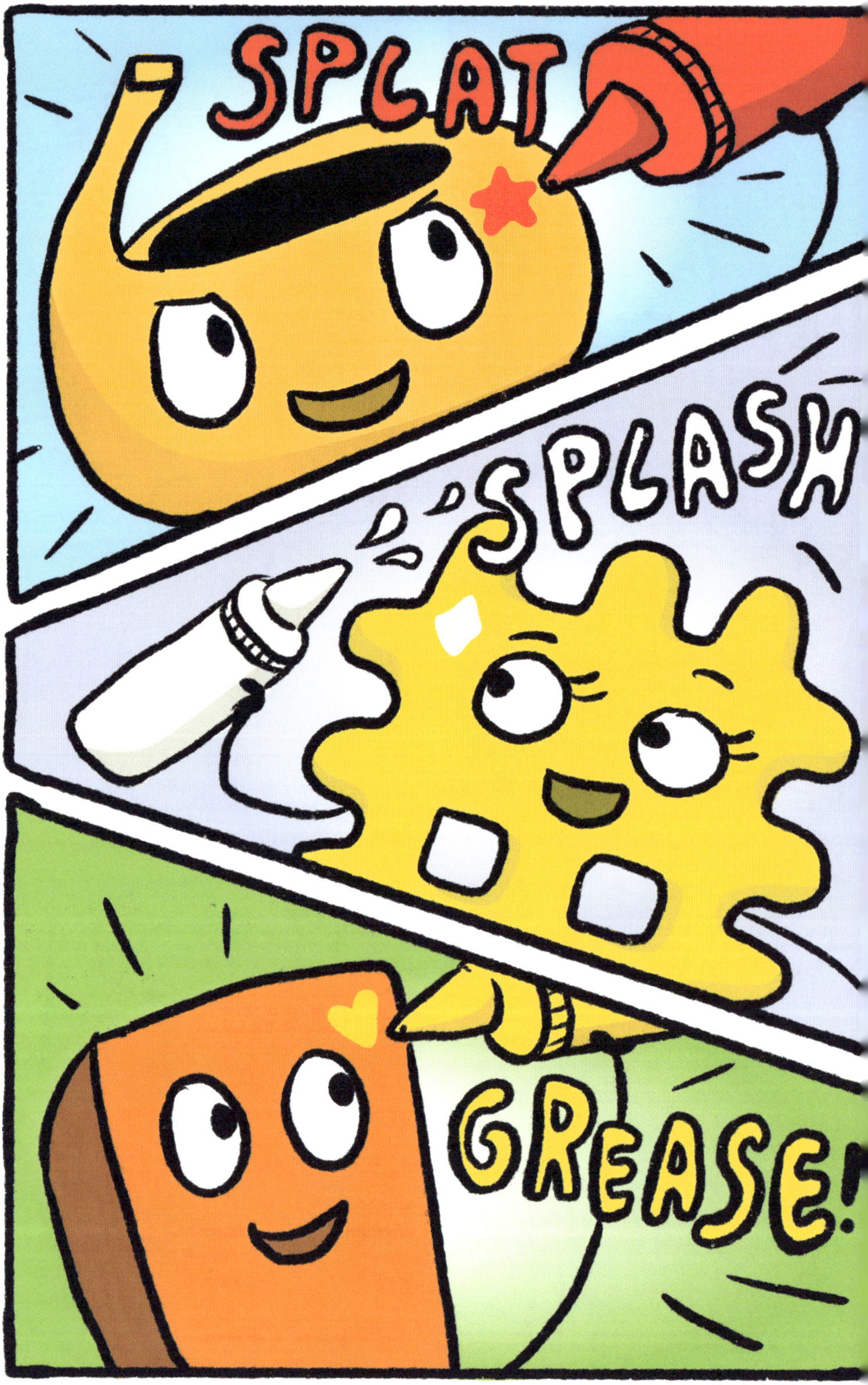
SPLAT
SPLASH
GREASE!

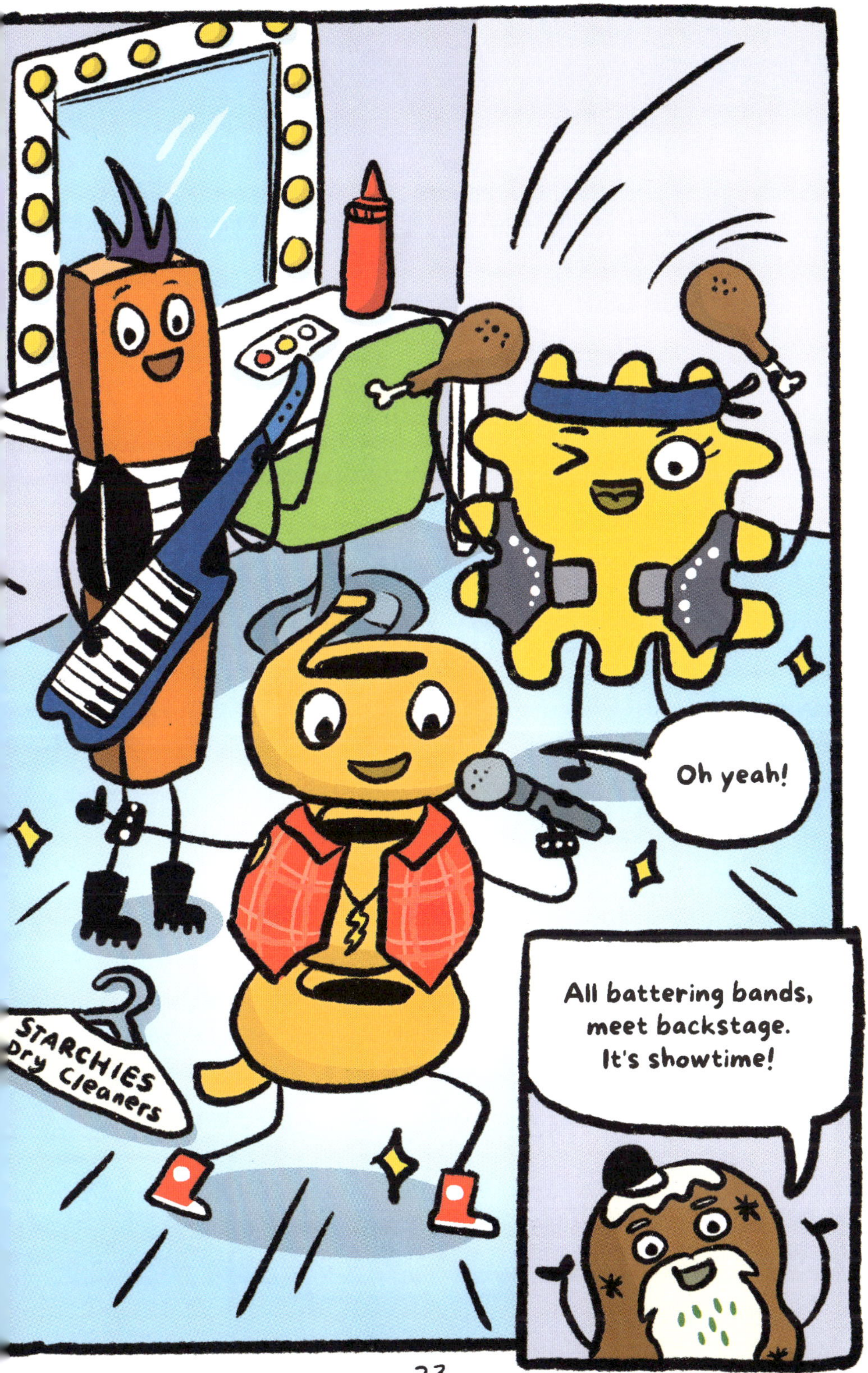
Oh yeah!
STARCHIES Dry Cleaners
All battering bands, meet backstage. It's showtime!

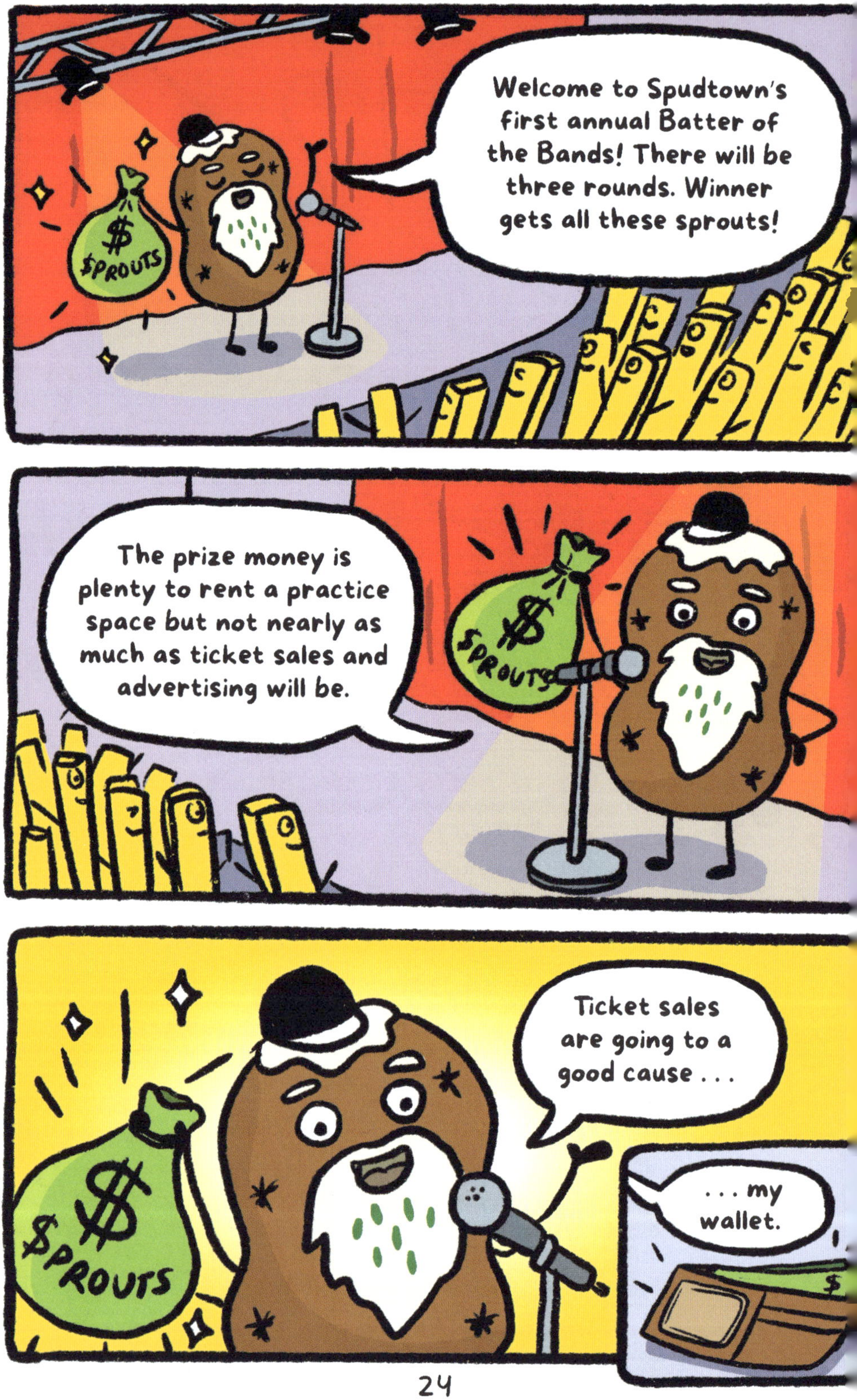
Welcome to Spudtown's first annual Batter of the Bands! There will be three rounds. Winner gets all these sprouts!
$PROUTS
The prize money is plenty to rent a practice space but not nearly as much as ticket sales and advertising will be.
$PROUTS
Ticket sales are going to a good cause . . .
$PROUTS
. . . my wallet.

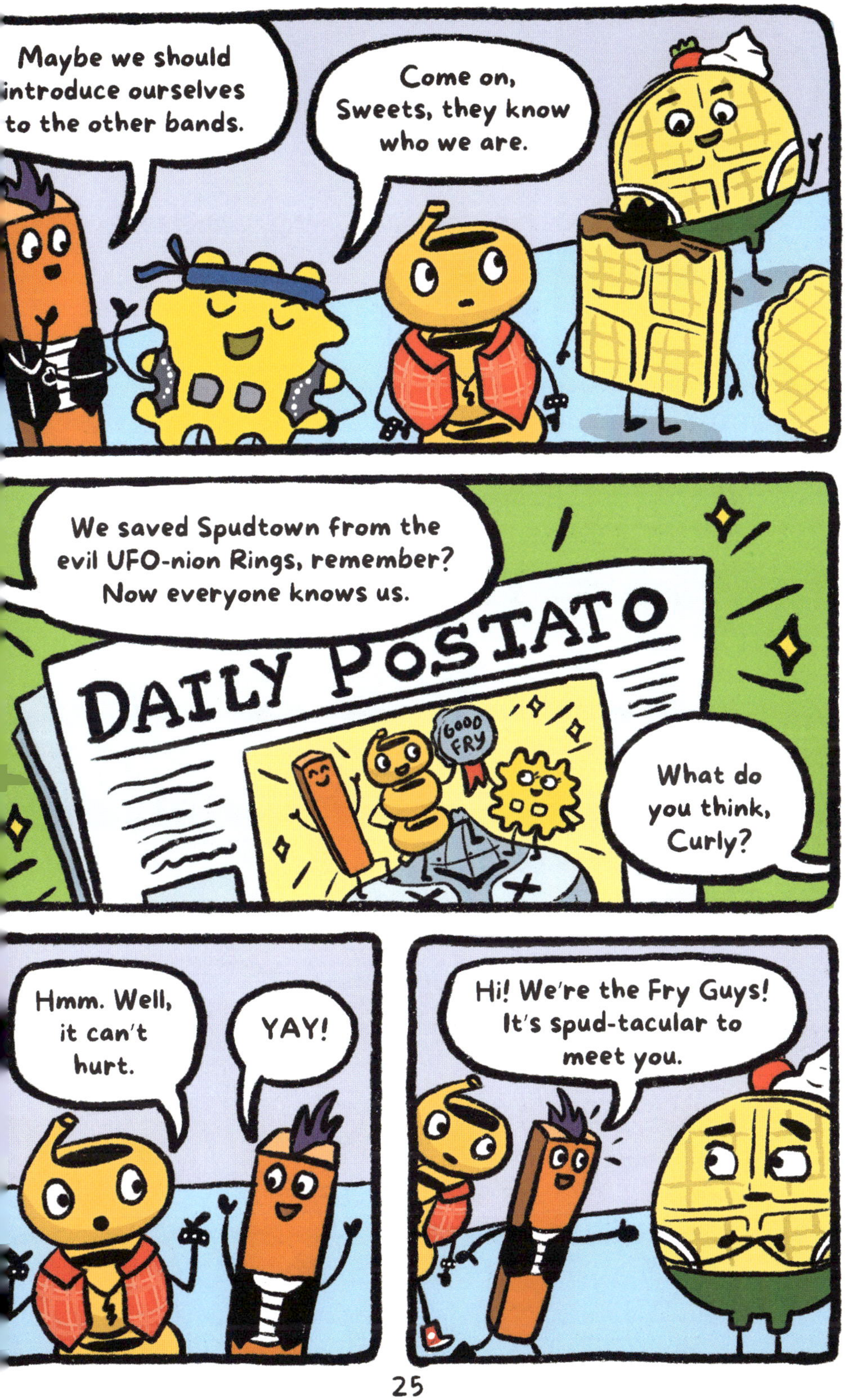

Maybe we should introduce ourselves to the other bands.
Come on, Sweets, they know who we are.
We saved Spudtown from the evil UFO-nion Rings, remember? Now everyone knows us.
DAILY POSTATO
GOOD FRY
What do you think, Curly?
Hmm. Well, it can't hurt.
YAY!
Hi! We're the Fry Guys! It's spud-tacular to meet you.

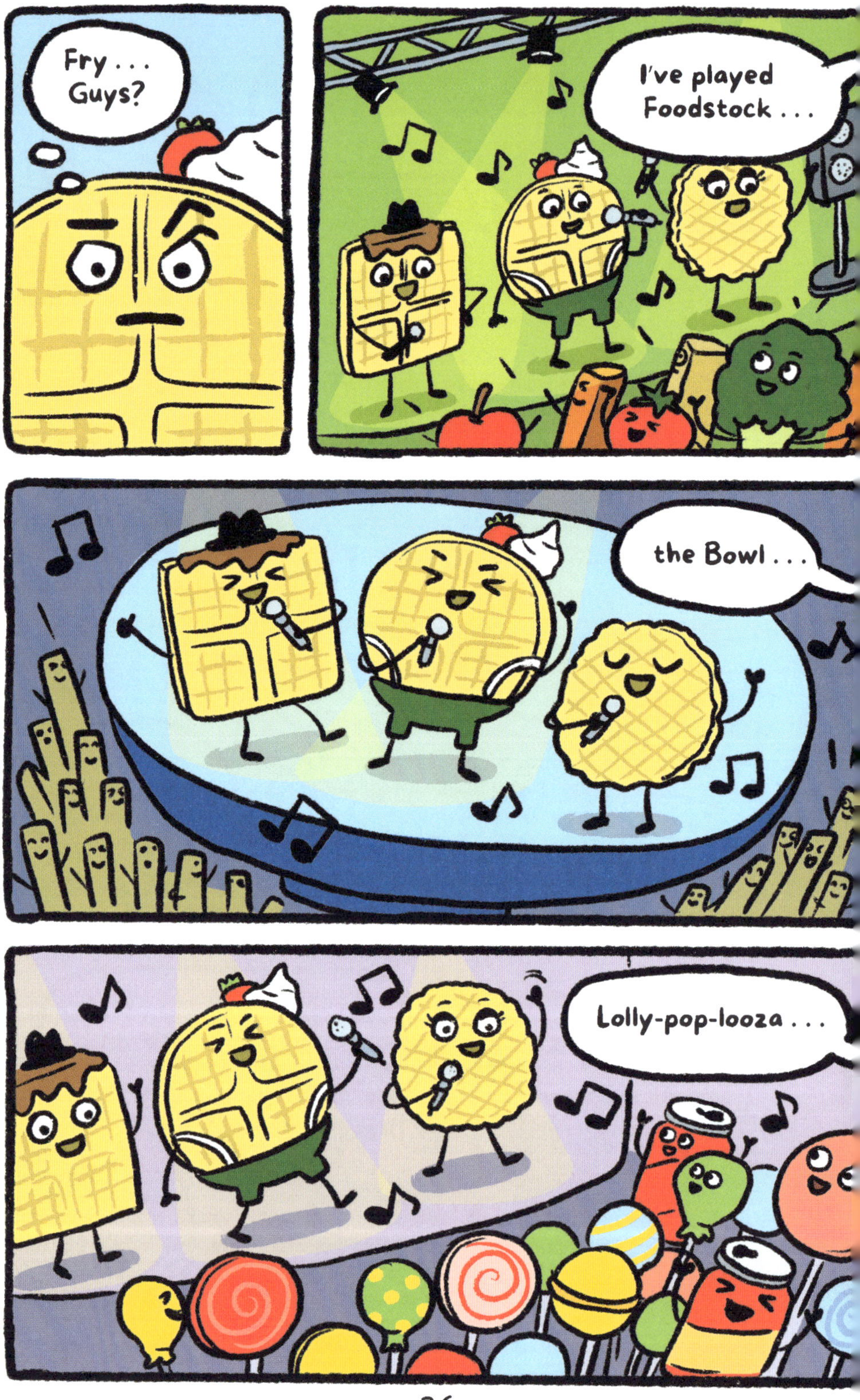
Fry . . . Guys?
I've played Foodstock . . .
the Bowl . . .
Lolly-pop-looza . . .

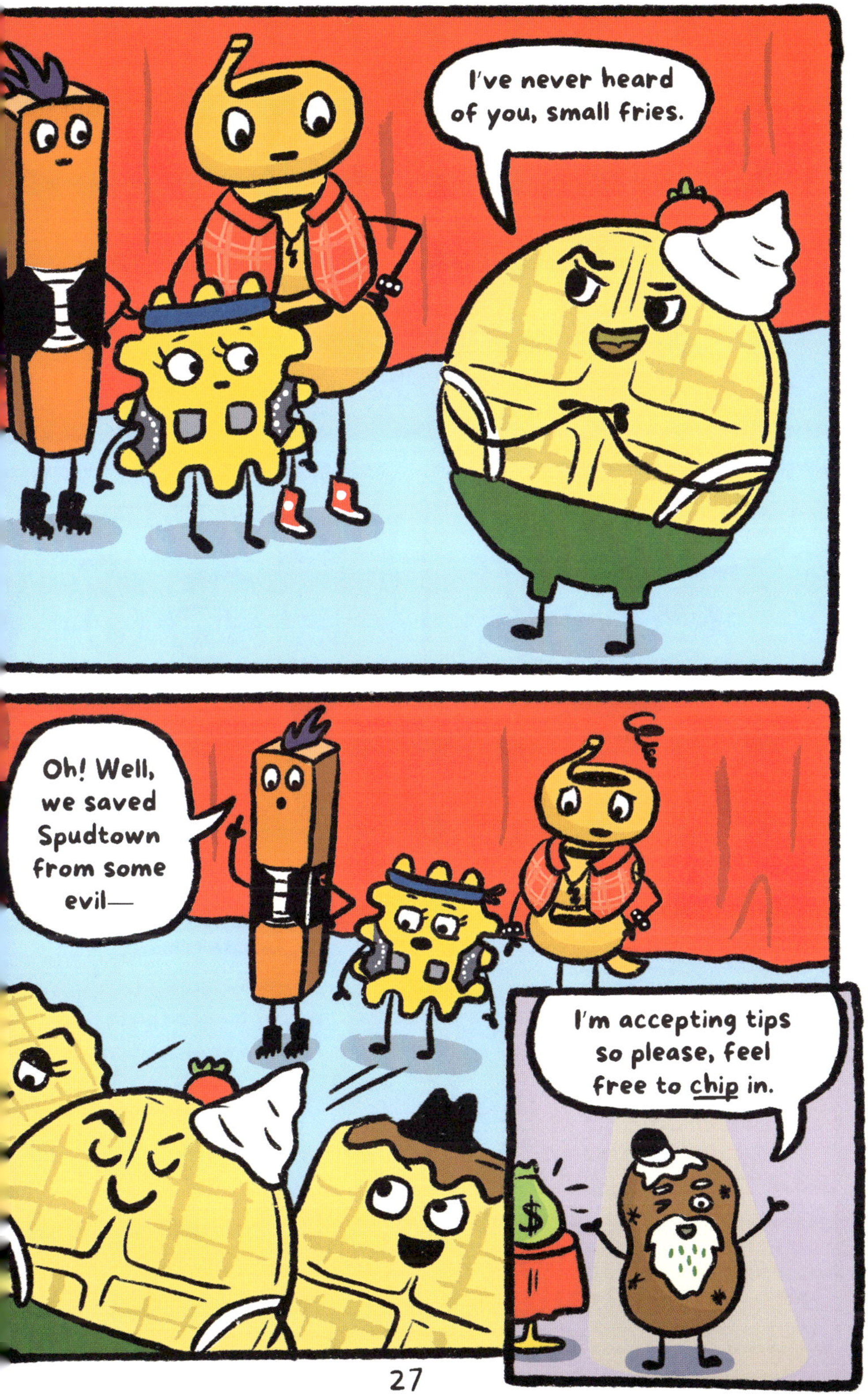
I've never heard of you, small fries.
Oh! Well, we saved Spudtown from some evil—
I'm accepting tips so please, feel free to chip in.

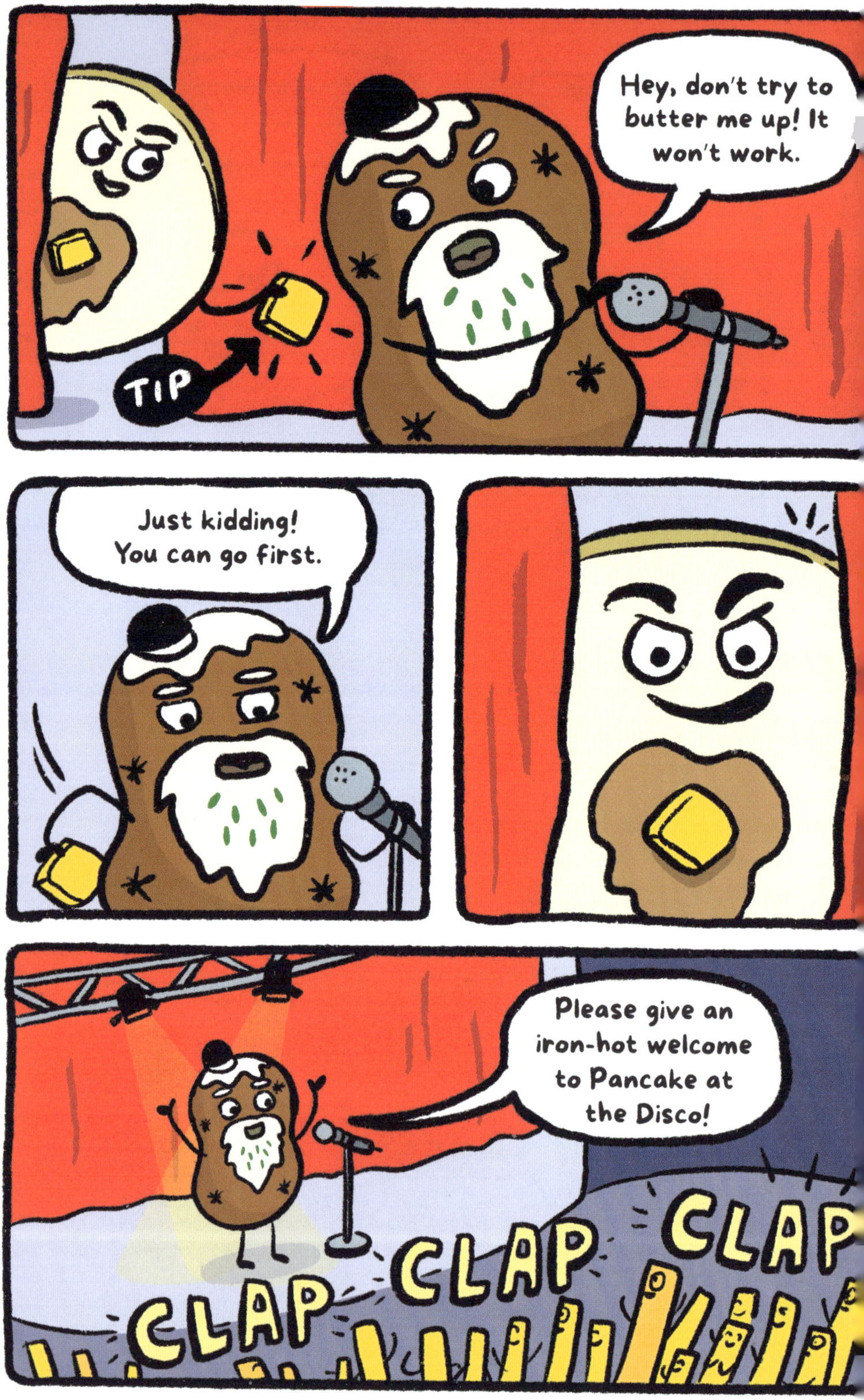
Hey, don't try to butter me up! It won't work.
TIP
Just kidding! You can go first.
Please give an iron-hot welcome to Pancake at the Disco!
CLAP CLAP CLAP

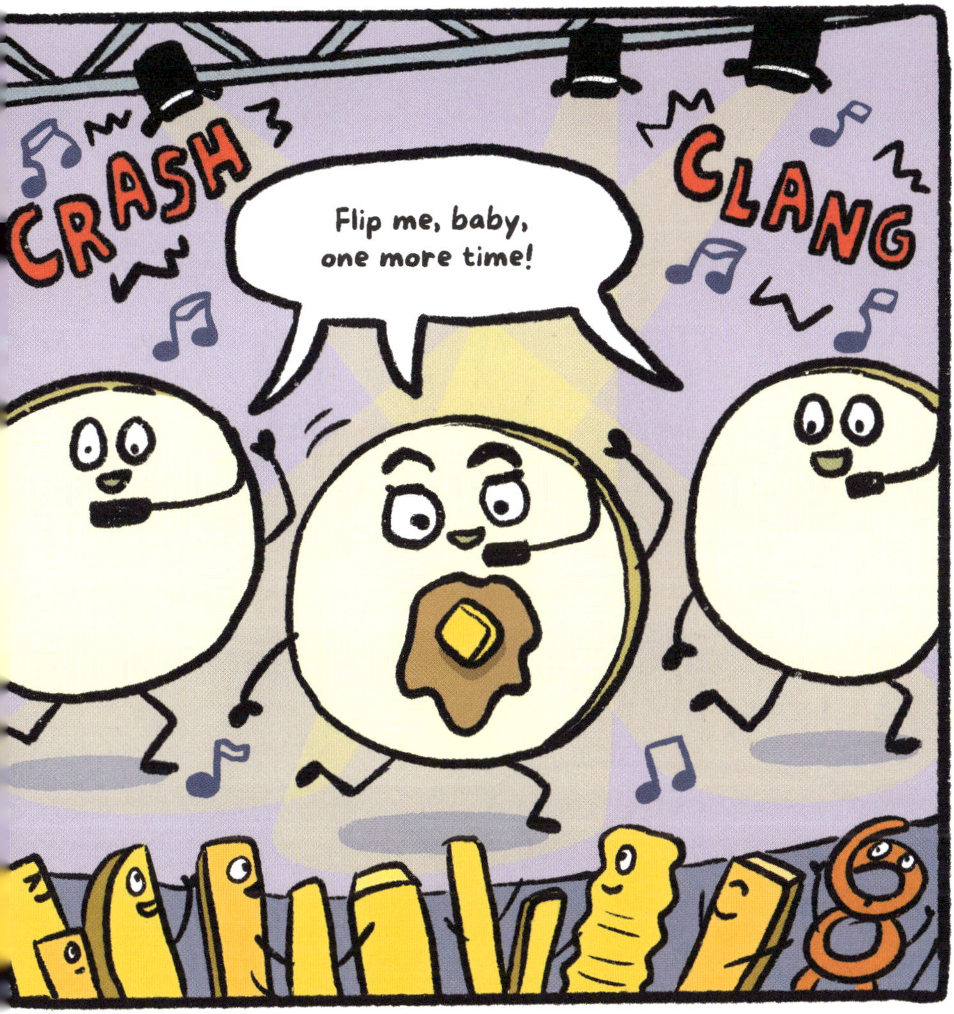
CRASH
CLANG
Flip me, baby, one more time!

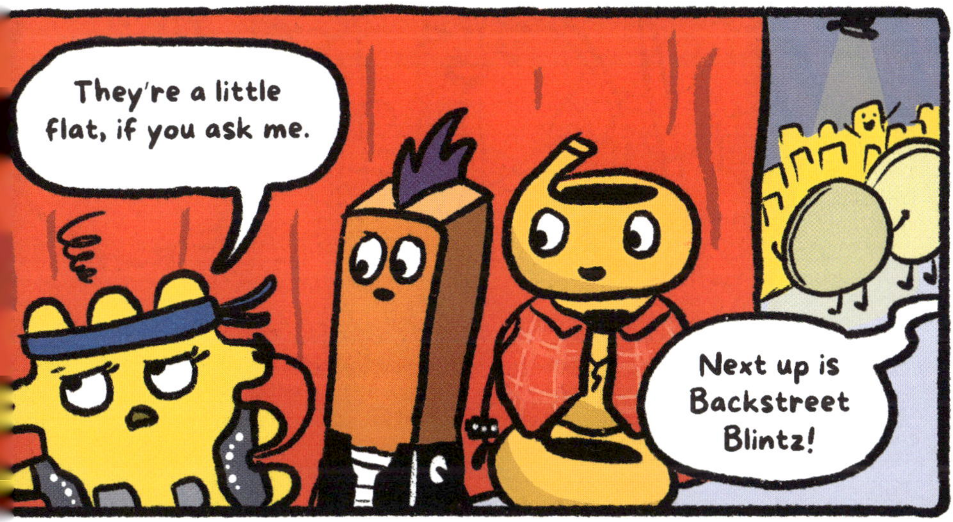
They're a little flat, if you ask me.
Next up is Backstreet Blintz!

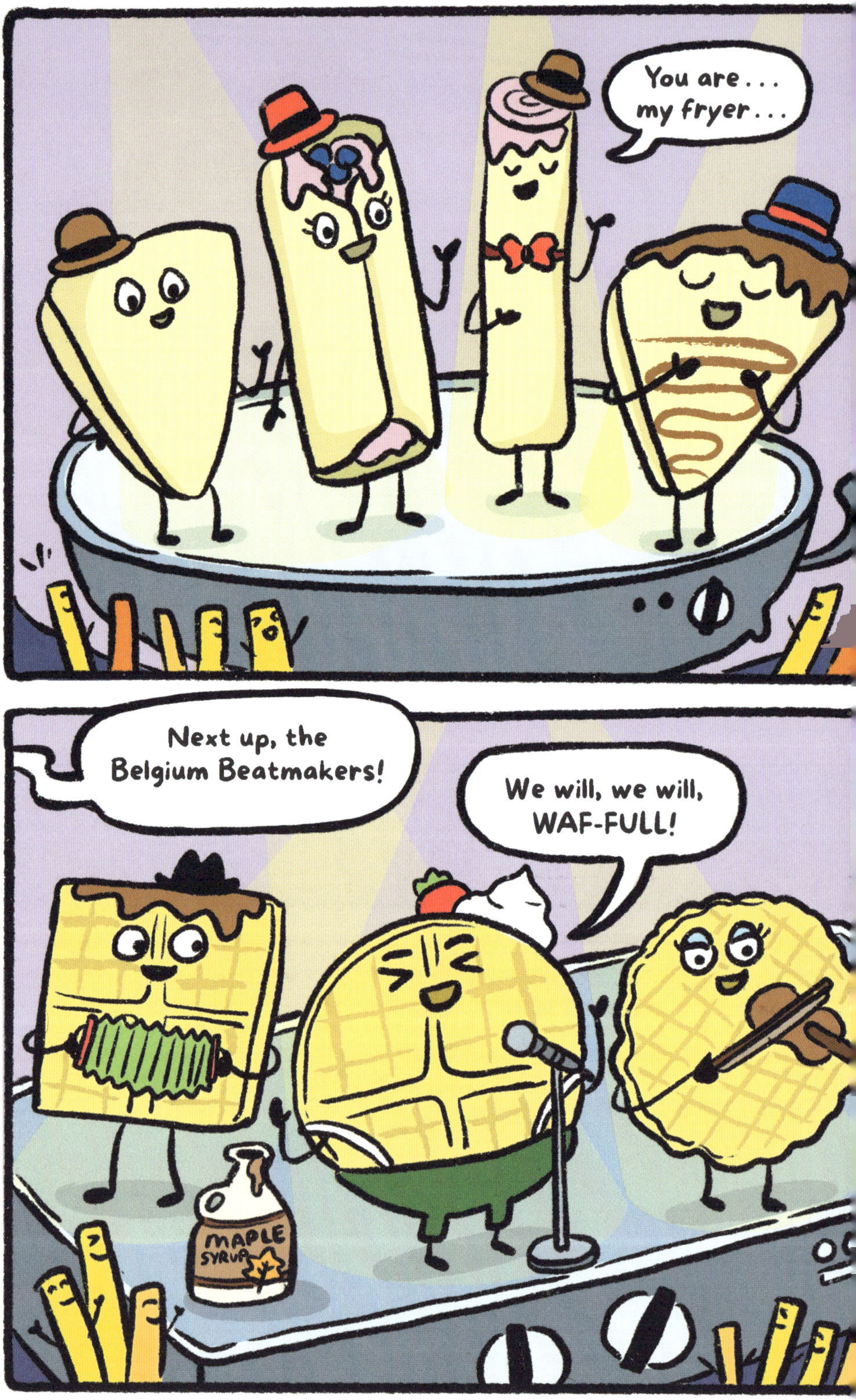
You are . . . my fryer . . .
Next up, the Belgium Beatmakers!
We will, we will, WAF-FULL!
MAPLE SYRUP

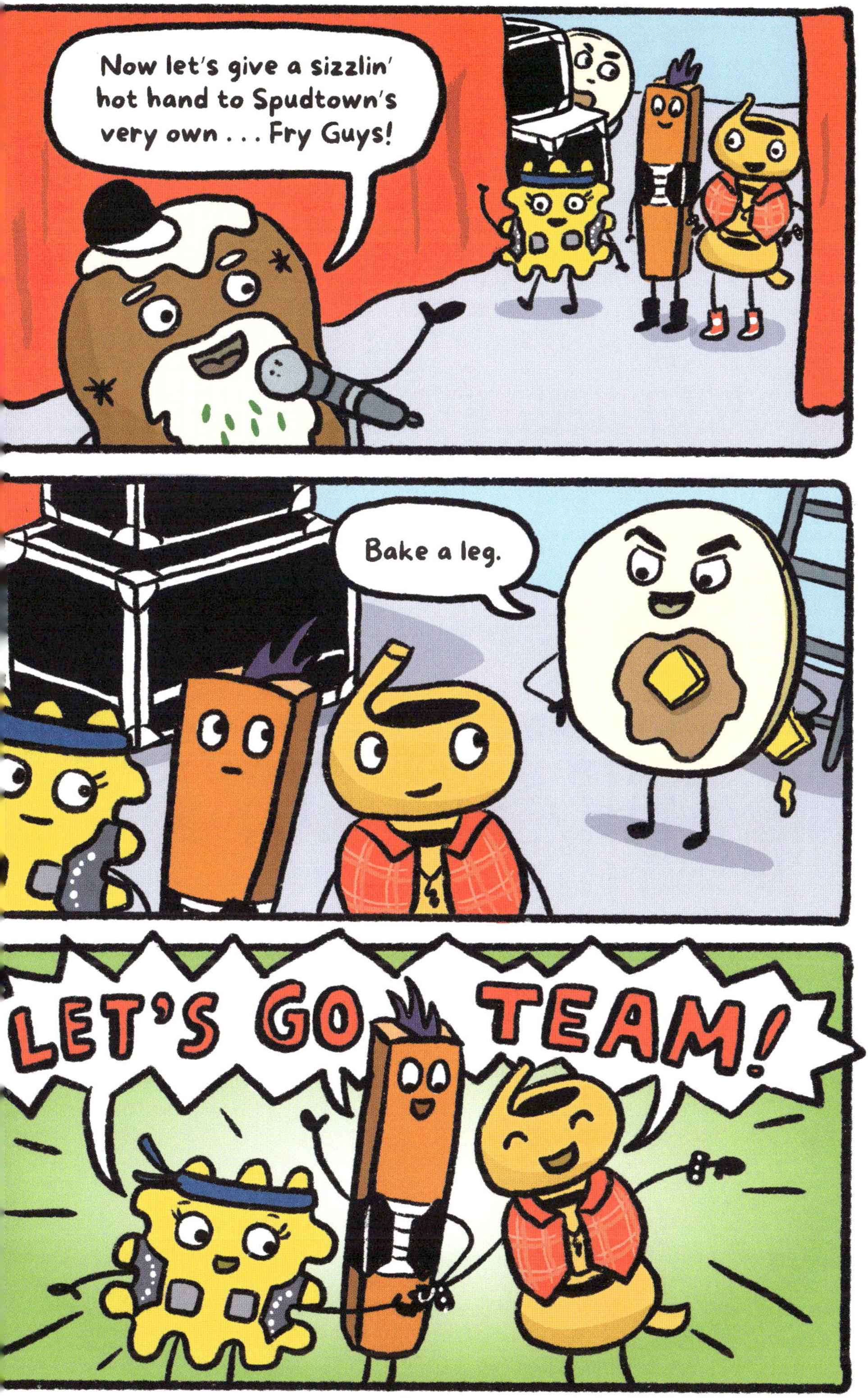
Now let's give a sizzlin' hot hand to Spudtown's very own . . . Fry Guys!
Bake a leg.
LET'S GO TEAM!

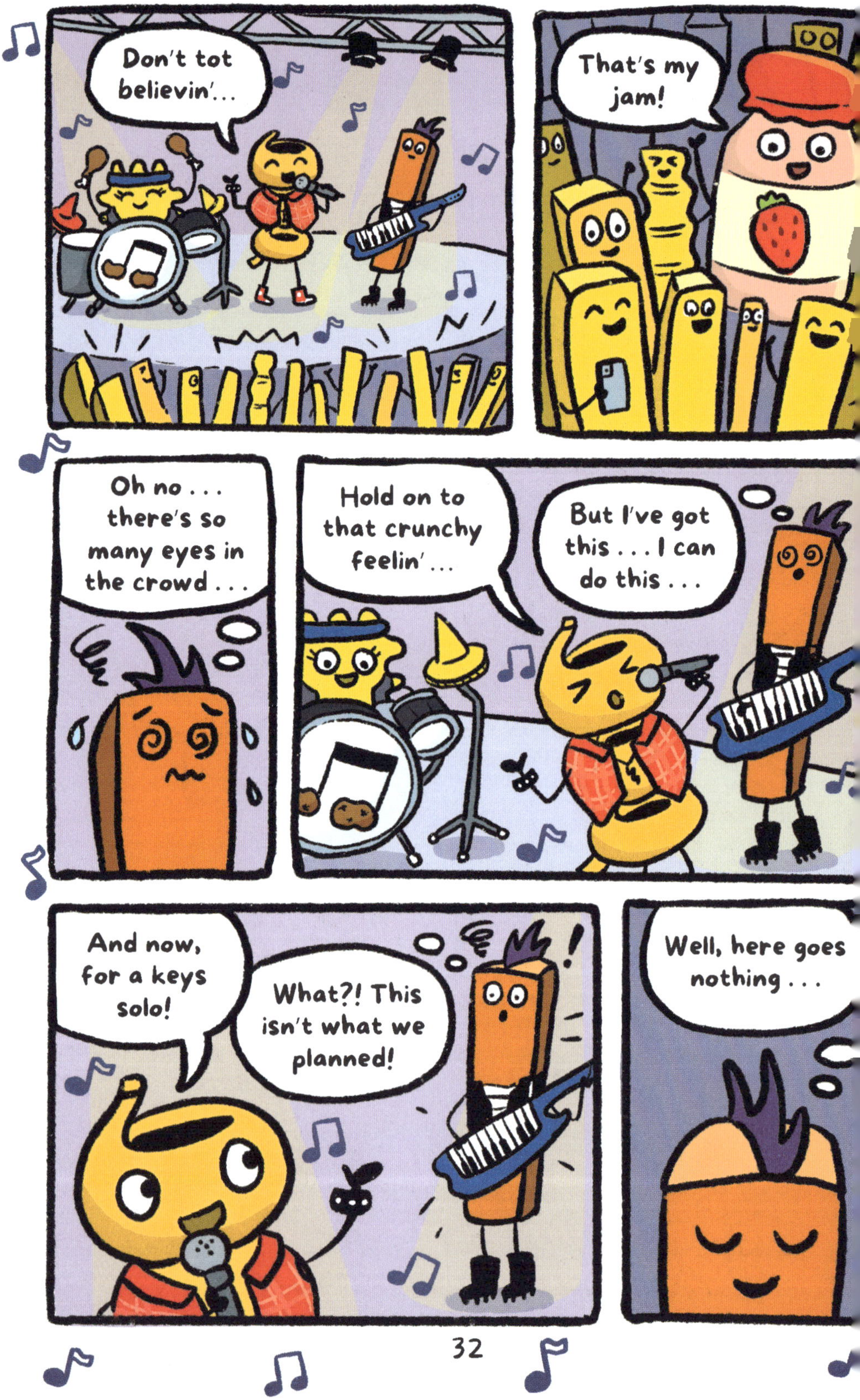
Don't tot believin'...
That's my jam!
Oh no . . . there's so many eyes in the crowd . . .
Hold on to that crunchy feelin' . . .
But I've got this . . . I can do this . . .
And now, for a keys solo!
What?! This isn't what we planned!
Well, here goes nothing . . .

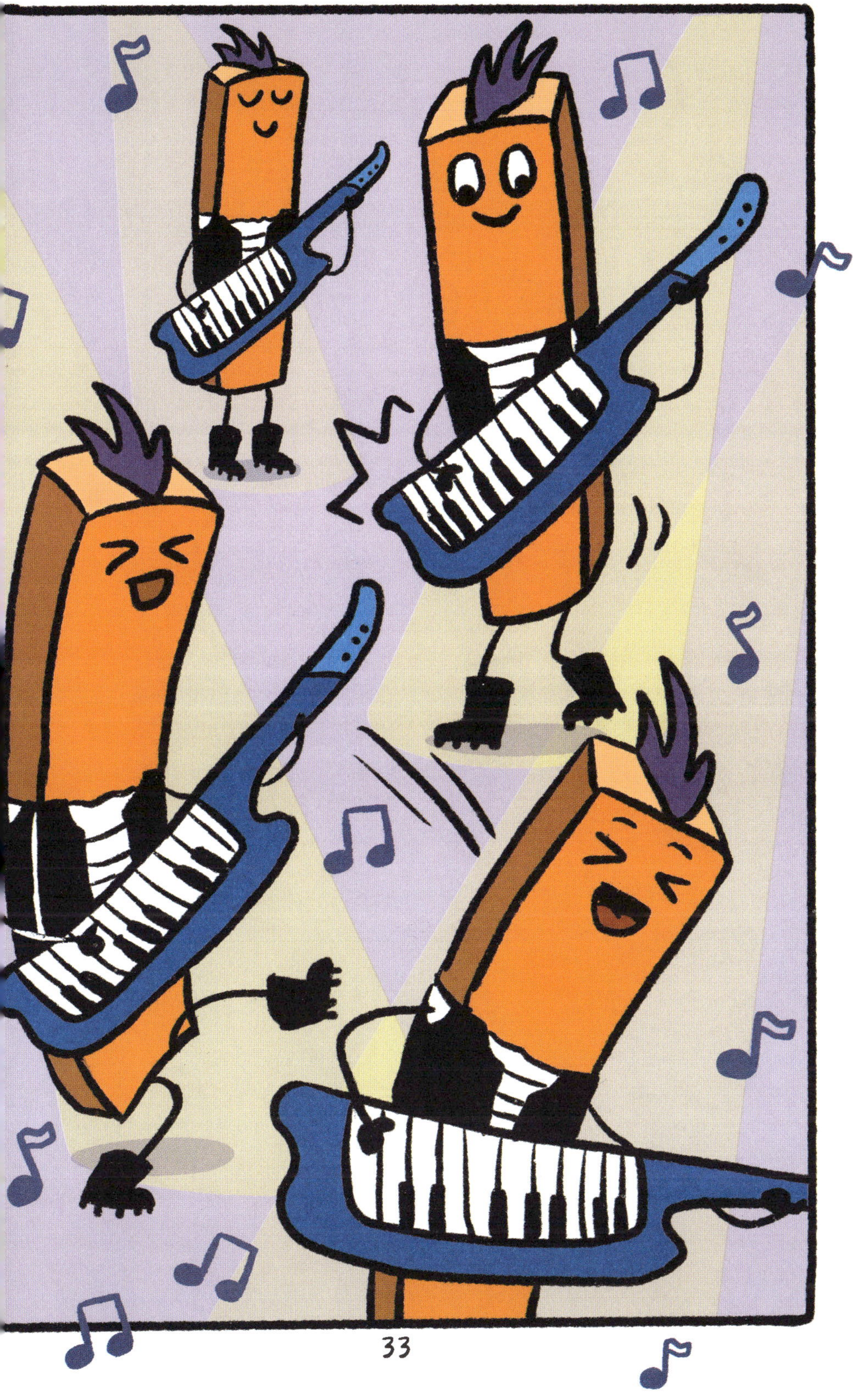

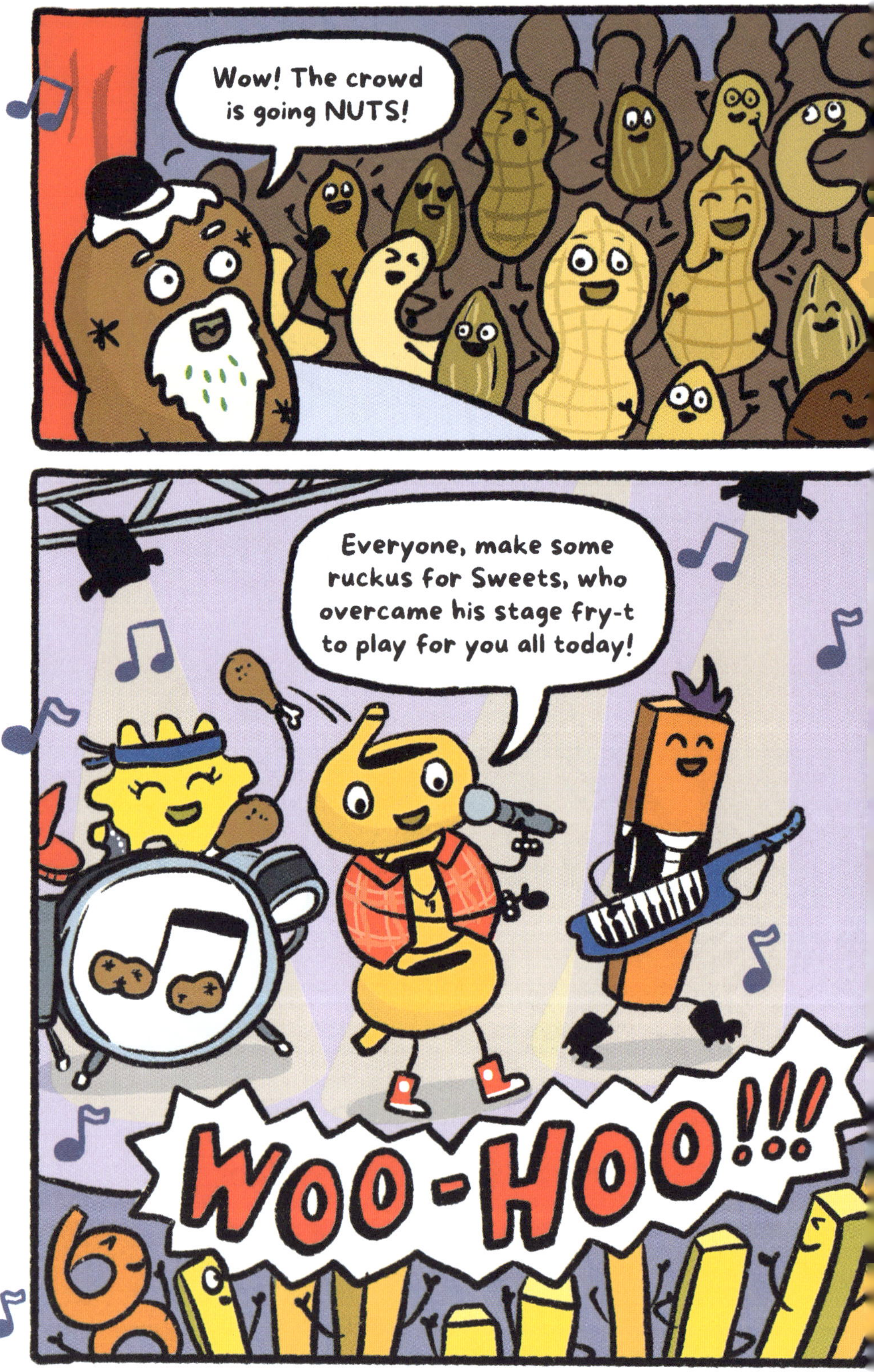
Wow! The crowd is going NUTS!
Everyone, make some ruckus for Sweets, who overcame his stage fry-t to play for you all today!
WOO-HOO!!!

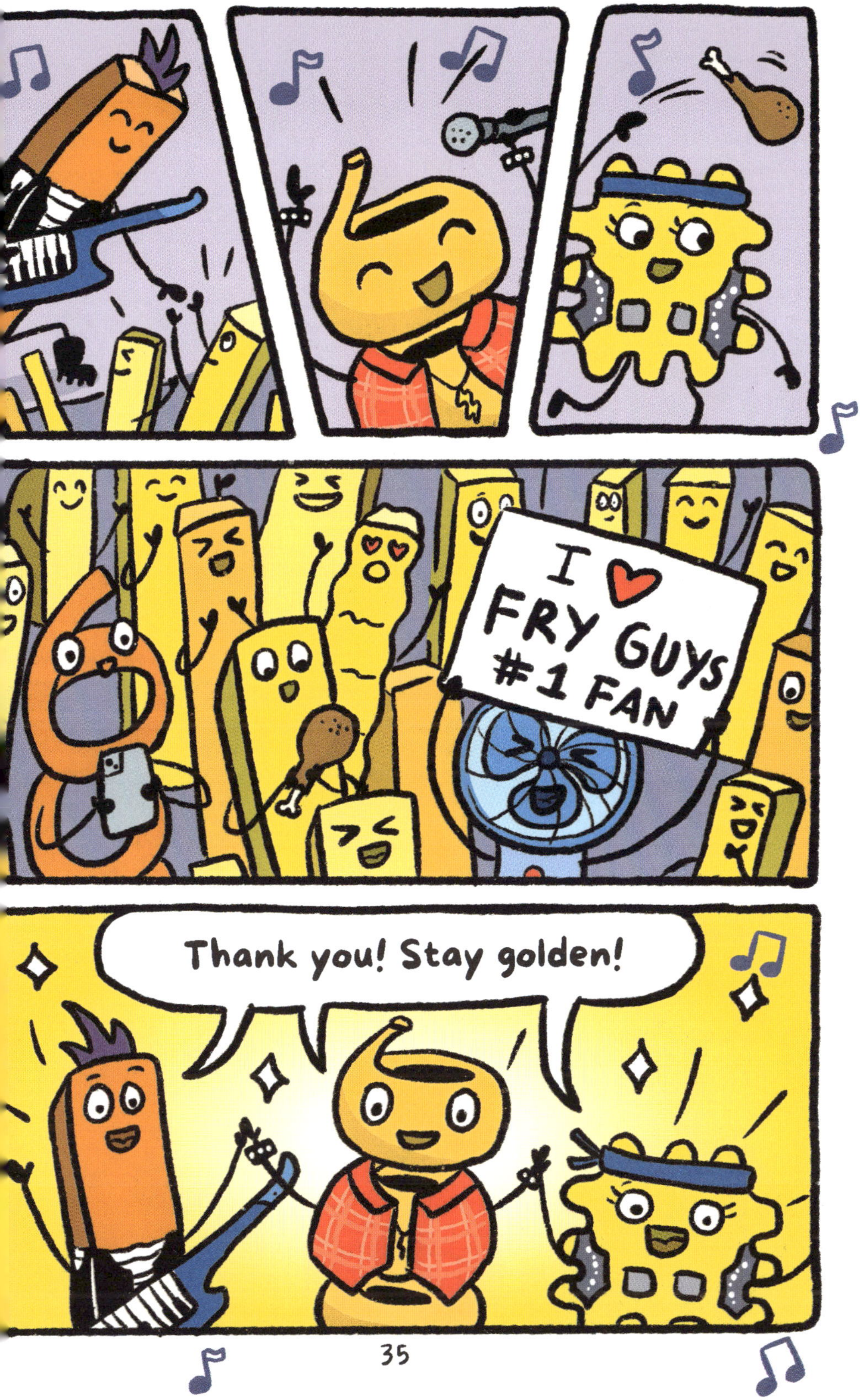
I ♥ FRY GUYS #1 FAN
Thank you! Stay golden!

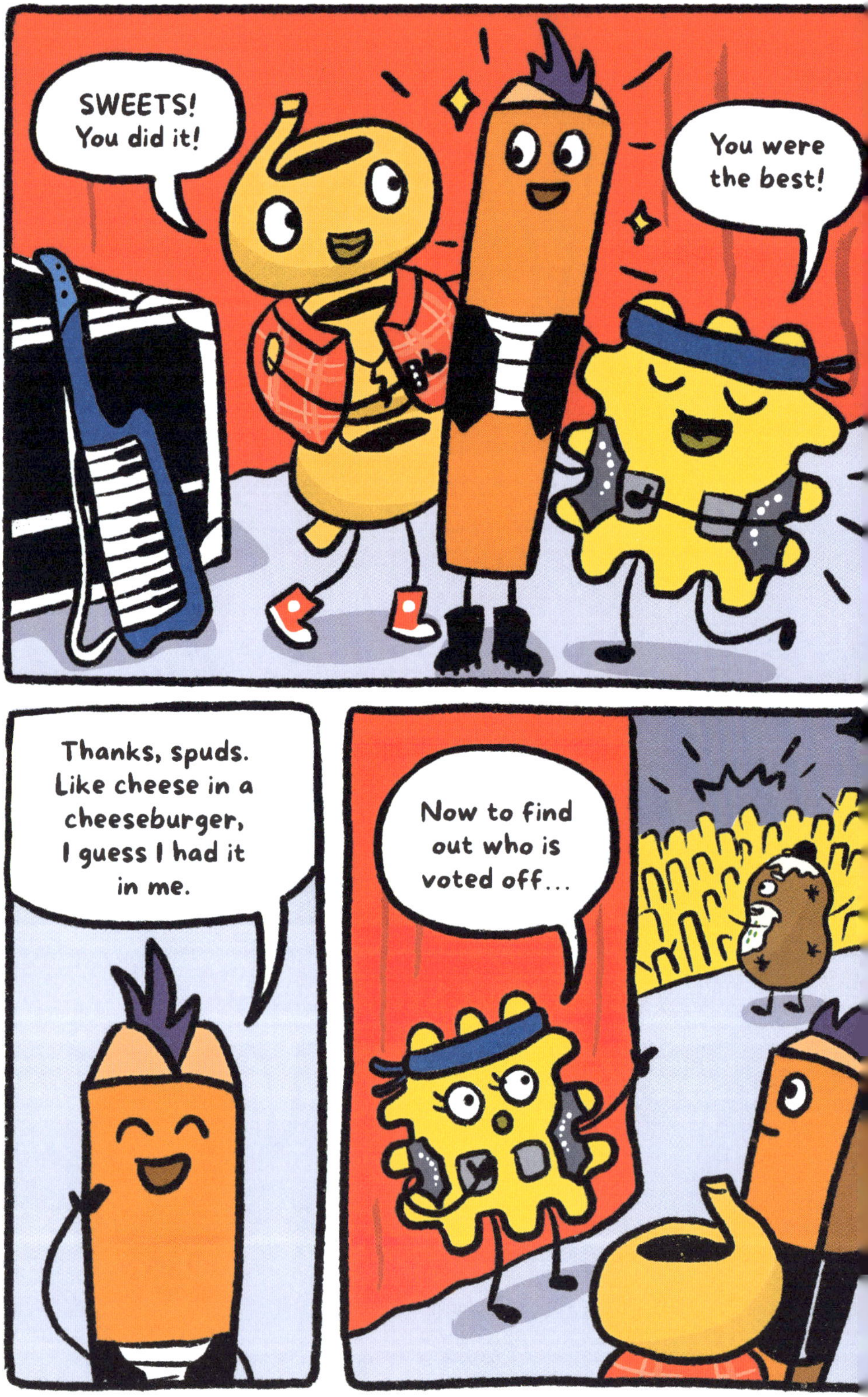
SWEETS! You did it!
You were the best!
Thanks, spuds. Like cheese in a cheeseburger, I guess I had it in me.
Now to find out who is voted off...

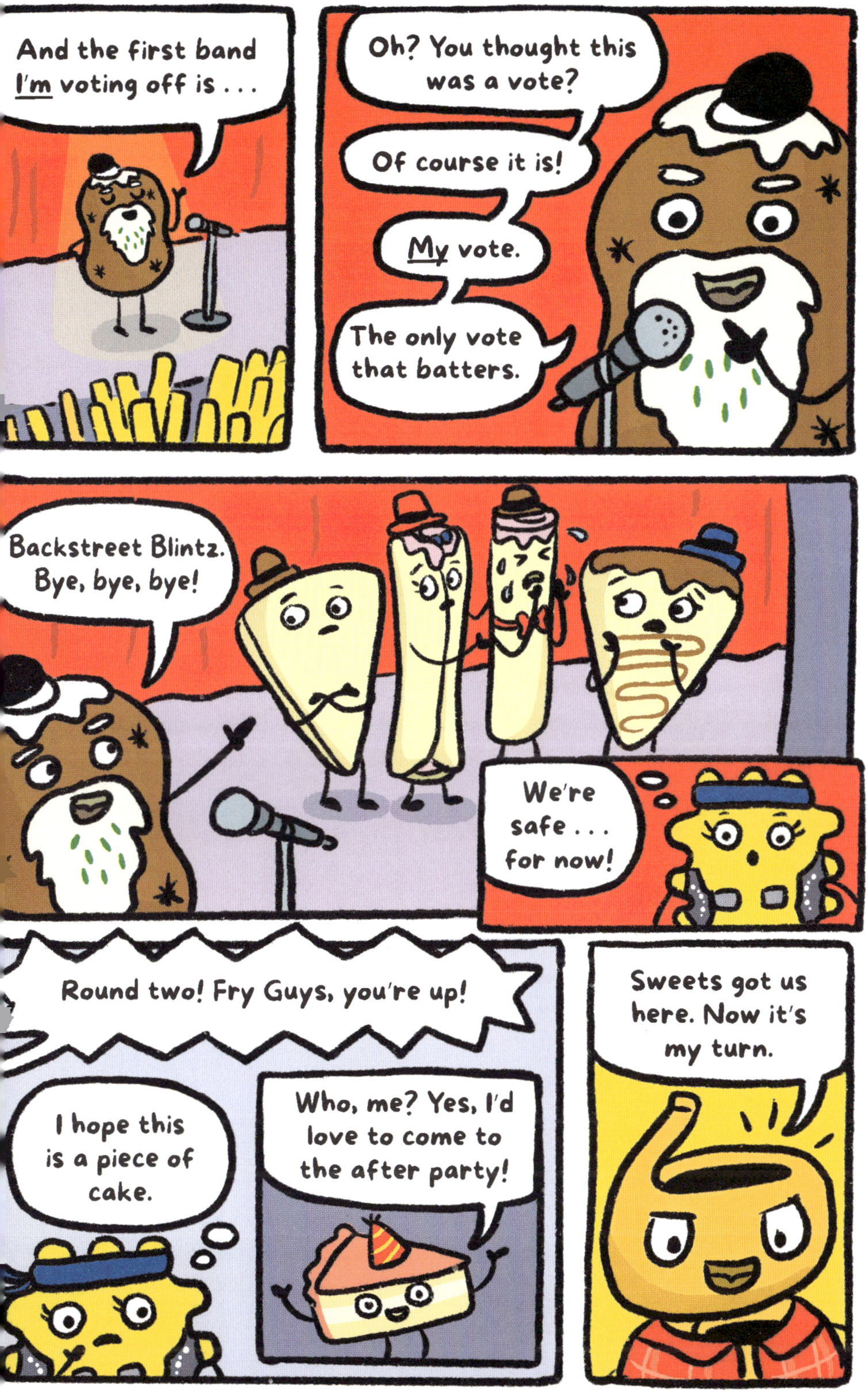
And the first band I'm voting off is . . .
Oh? You thought this was a vote?
Of course it is!
My vote.
The only vote that batters.
Backstreet Blintz. Bye, bye, bye!
We're safe . . . for now!
Round two! Fry Guys, you're up!
I hope this is a piece of cake.
Who, me? Yes, I'd love to come to the after party!
Sweets got us here. Now it's my turn.

CHAPTER 3 Batter's Up

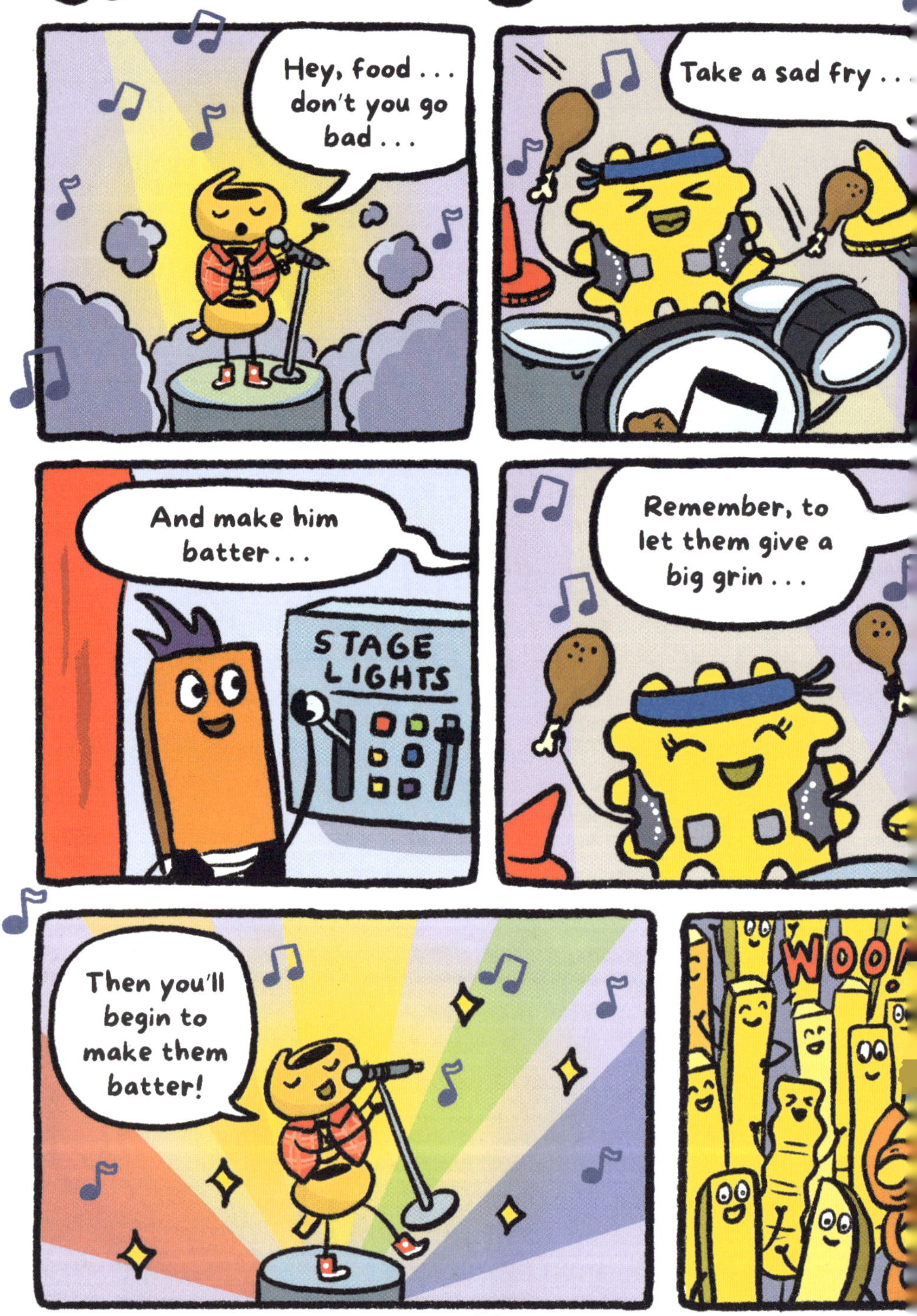

Hey, food . . . don't you go bad . . .
Take a sad fry . . .
And make him batter . . .
STAGE LIGHTS
Remember, to let them give a big grin . . .
Then you'll begin to make them batter!
WOO

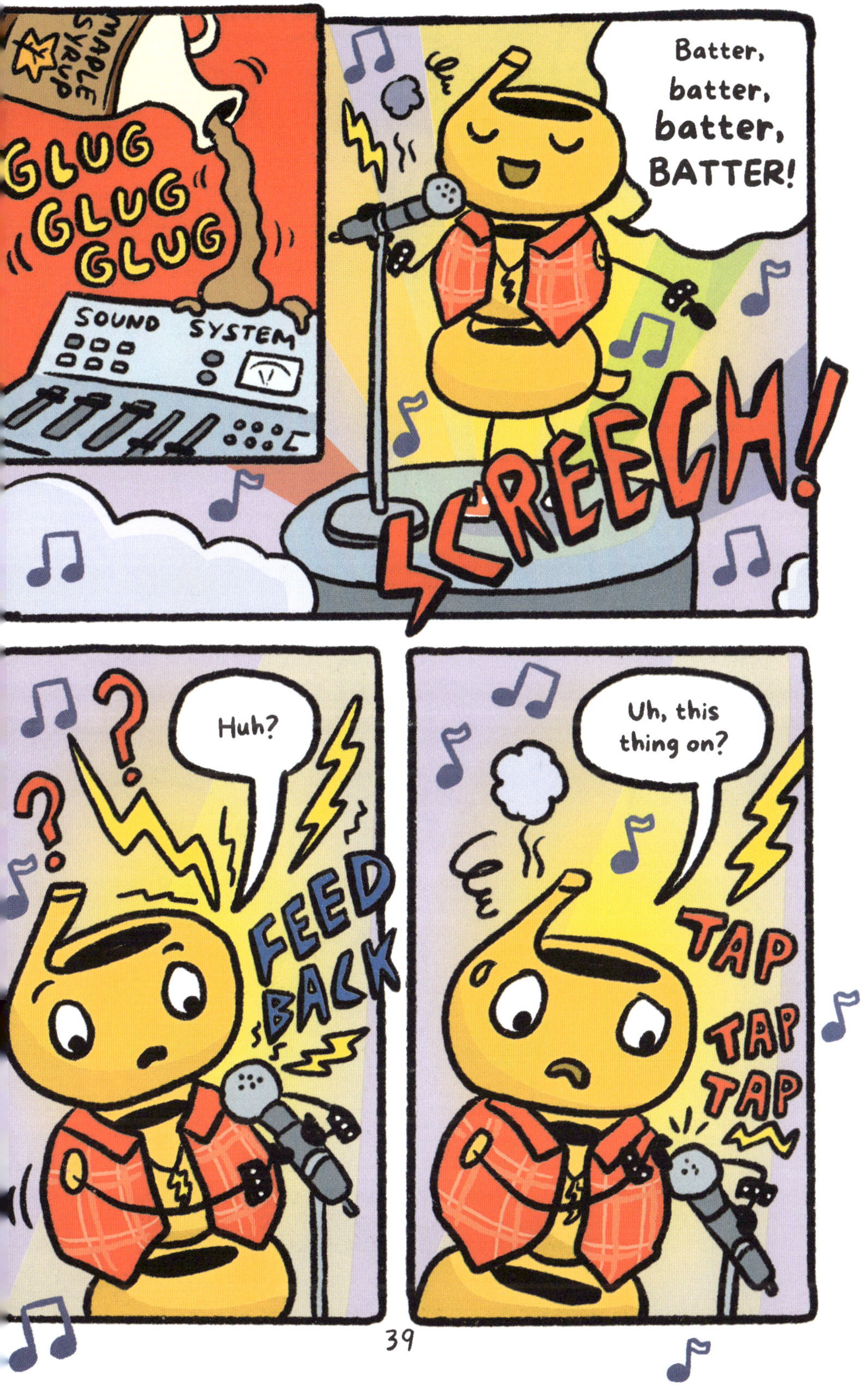
MAPLE SYRUP
GLUG GLUG GLUG
SOUND SYSTEM
Batter, batter, batter, BATTER!
SCREECH!
Huh?
FEED BACK
Uh, this thing on?
TAP TAP TAP

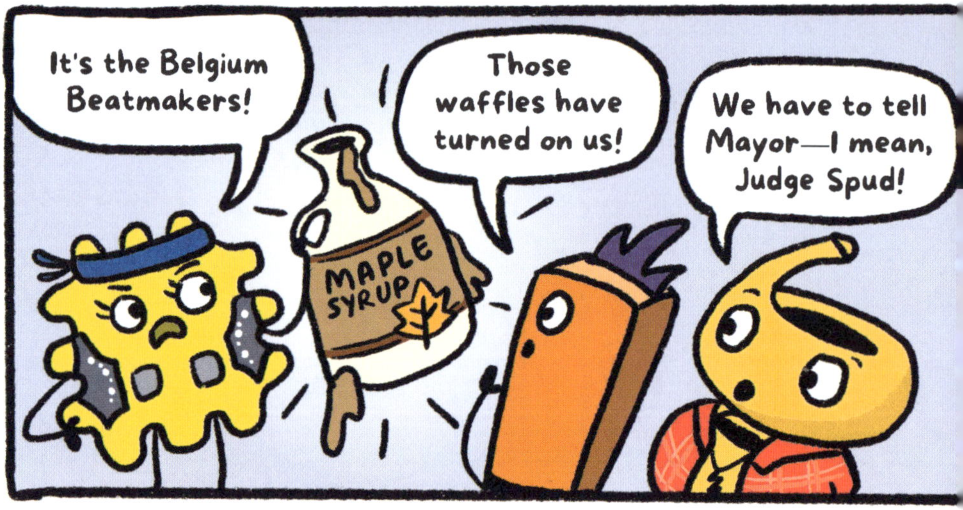
It's the Belgium Beatmakers!
Those waffles have turned on us!
We have to tell Mayor—I mean, Judge Spud!
MAPLE SYRUP

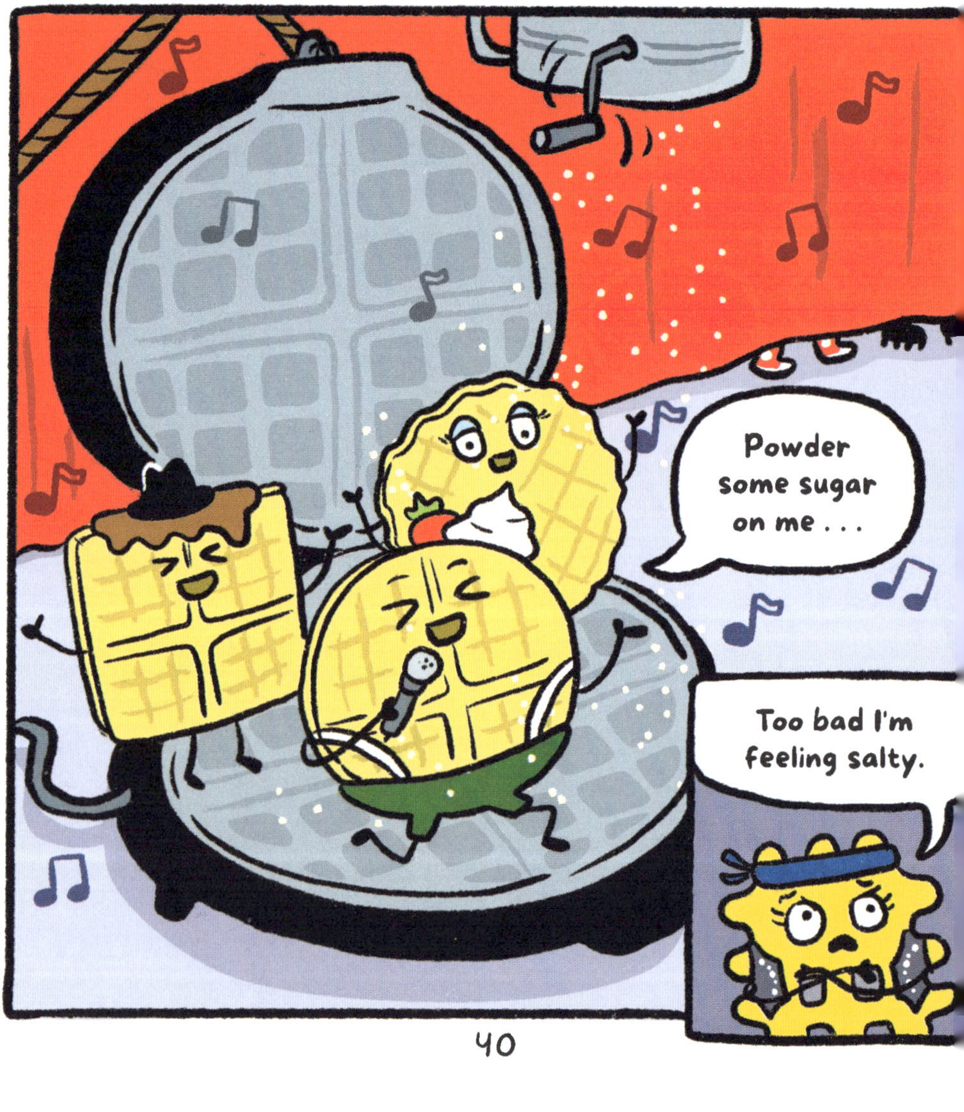
Powder some sugar on me . . .
Too bad I'm feeling salty.

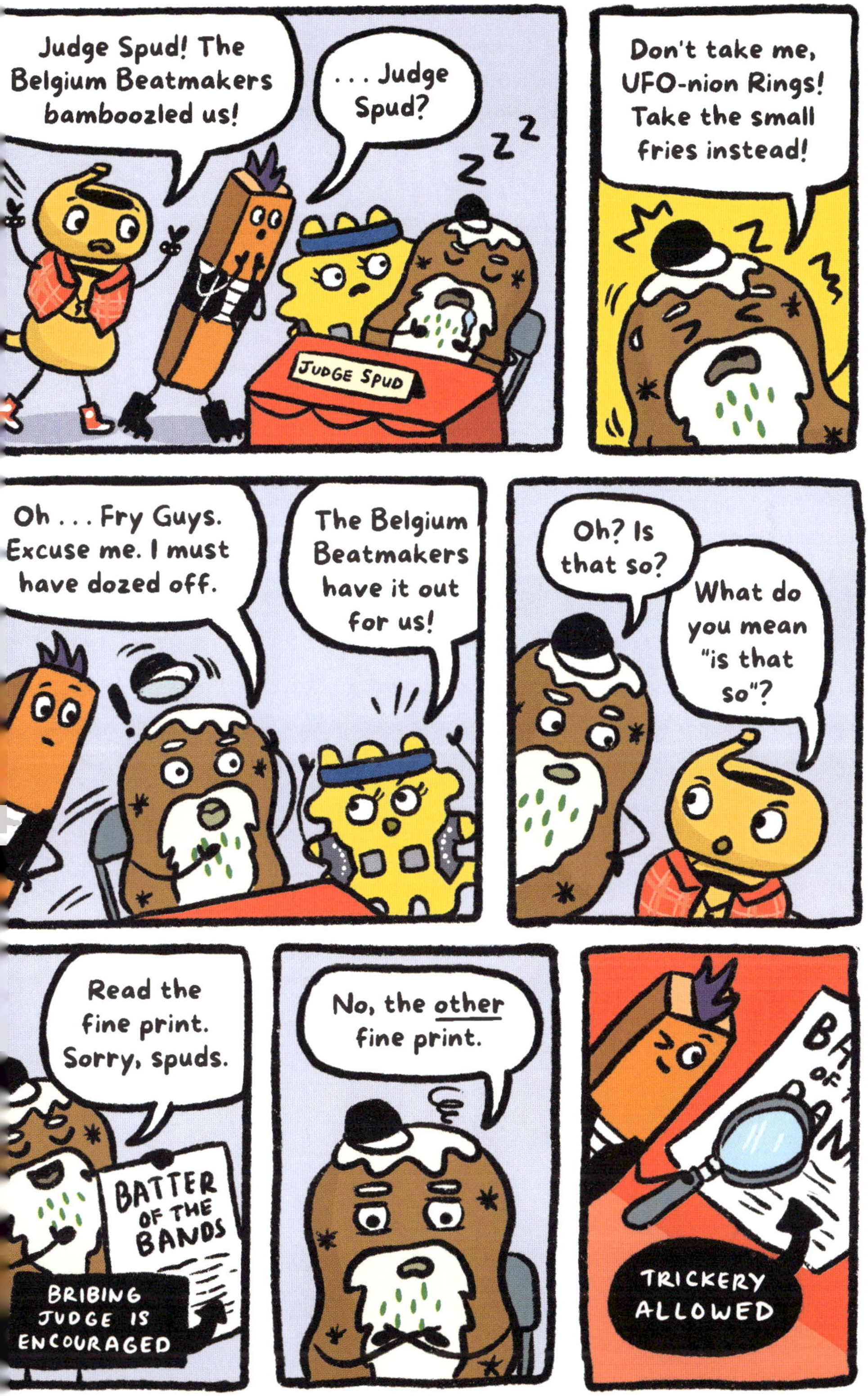
Judge Spud! The Belgium Beatmakers bamboozled us!
. . . Judge Spud?
Z Z Z
Don't take me, UFO-nion Rings! Take the small fries instead!
Z
Oh . . . Fry Guys. Excuse me. I must have dozed off.
The Belgium Beatmakers have it out for us!
Oh? Is that so?
What do you mean "is that so"?
Read the fine print. Sorry, spuds.
BATTER OF THE BANDS
BRIBING JUDGE IS ENCOURAGED
No, the other fine print.
TRICKERY ALLOWED

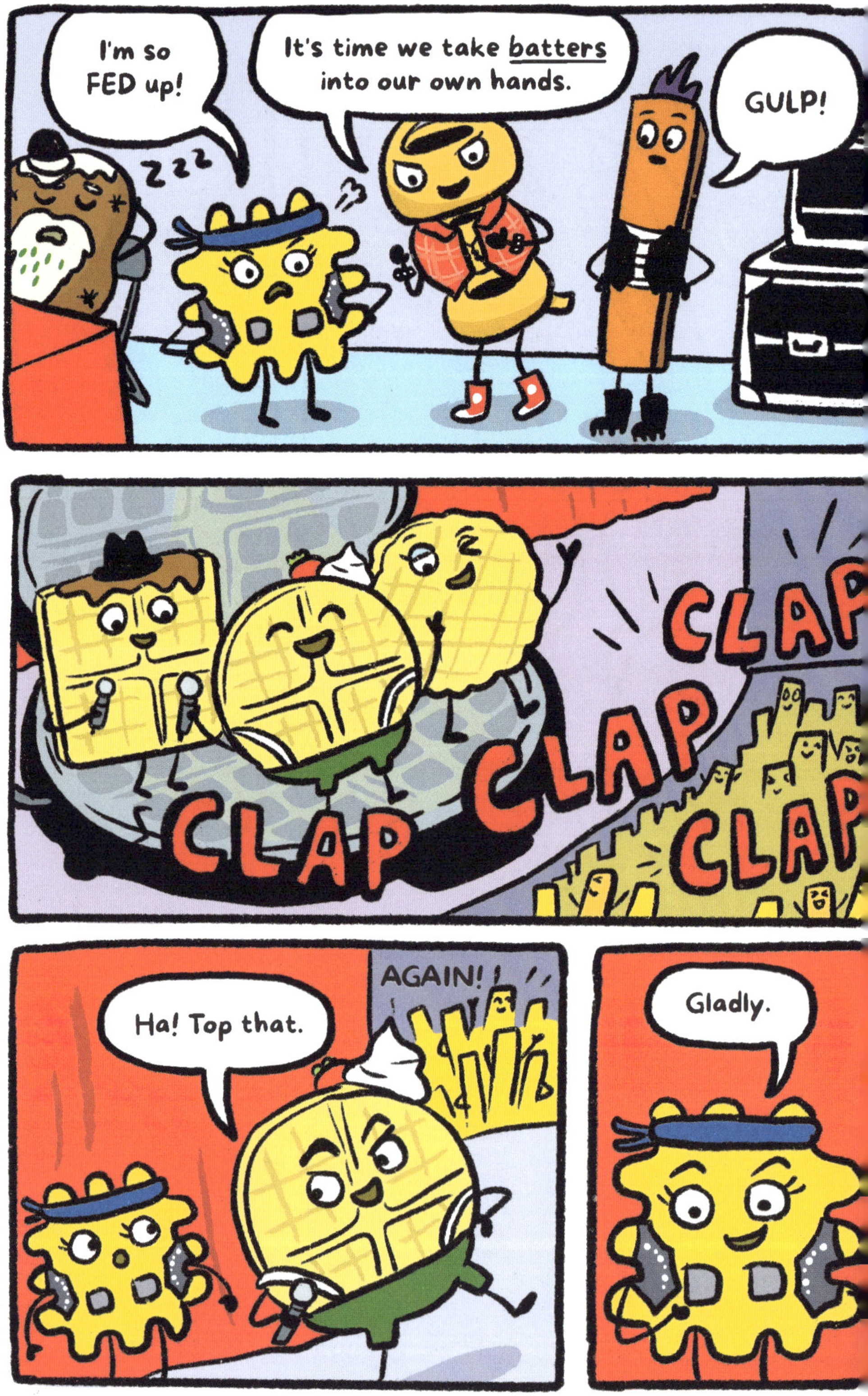
I'm so FED up!
It's time we take batters into our own hands.
Z Z Z
GULP!
CLAP
CLAP
CLAP
CLAP
Ha! Top that.
AGAIN!
Gladly.

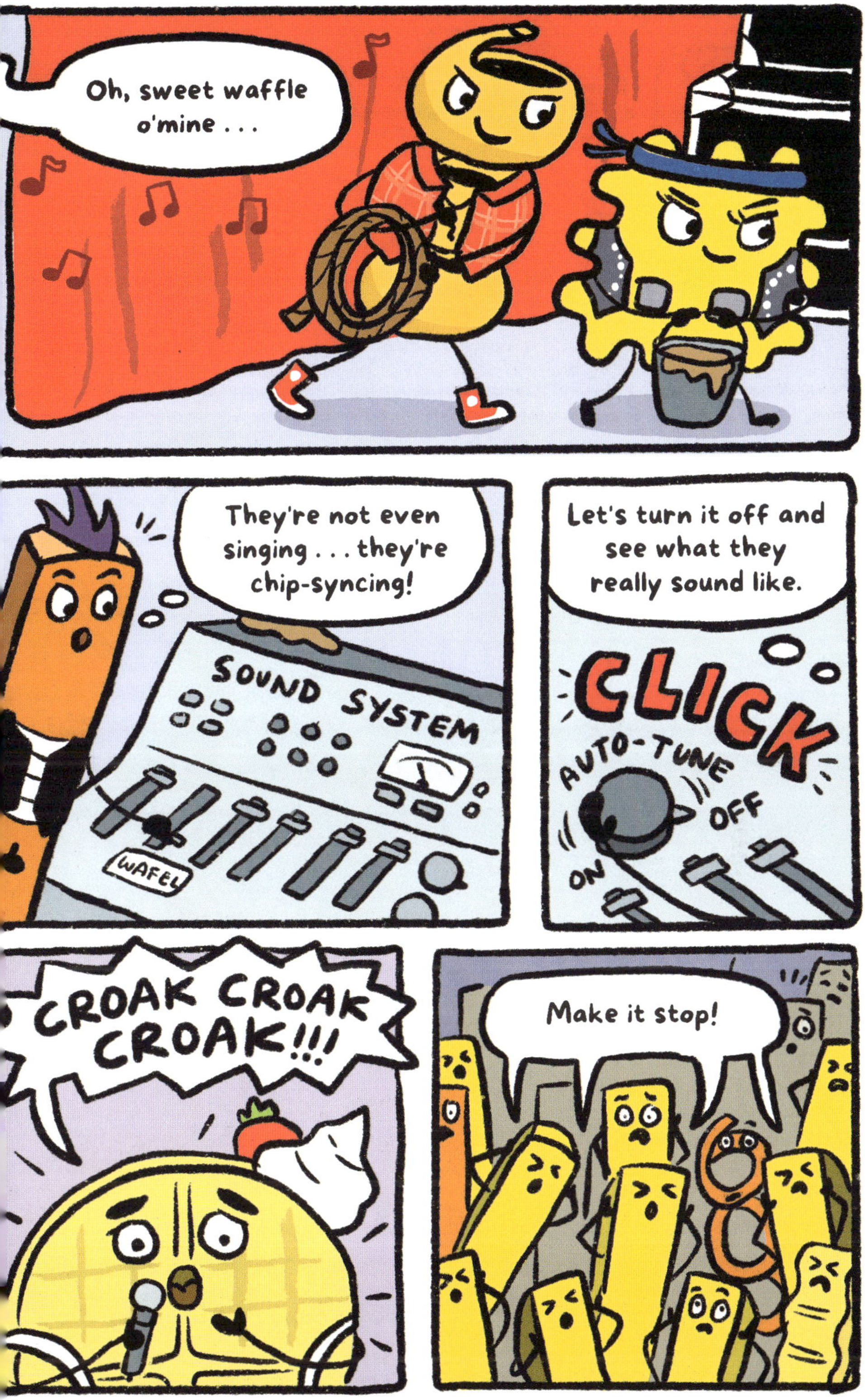
Oh, sweet waffle o'mine . . .
They're not even singing . . . they're chip-syncing!
SOUND SYSTEM
WAFEL
Let's turn it off and see what they really sound like.
CLICK
AUTO-TUNE
ON
OFF
CROAK CROAK CROAK!!!
Make it stop!

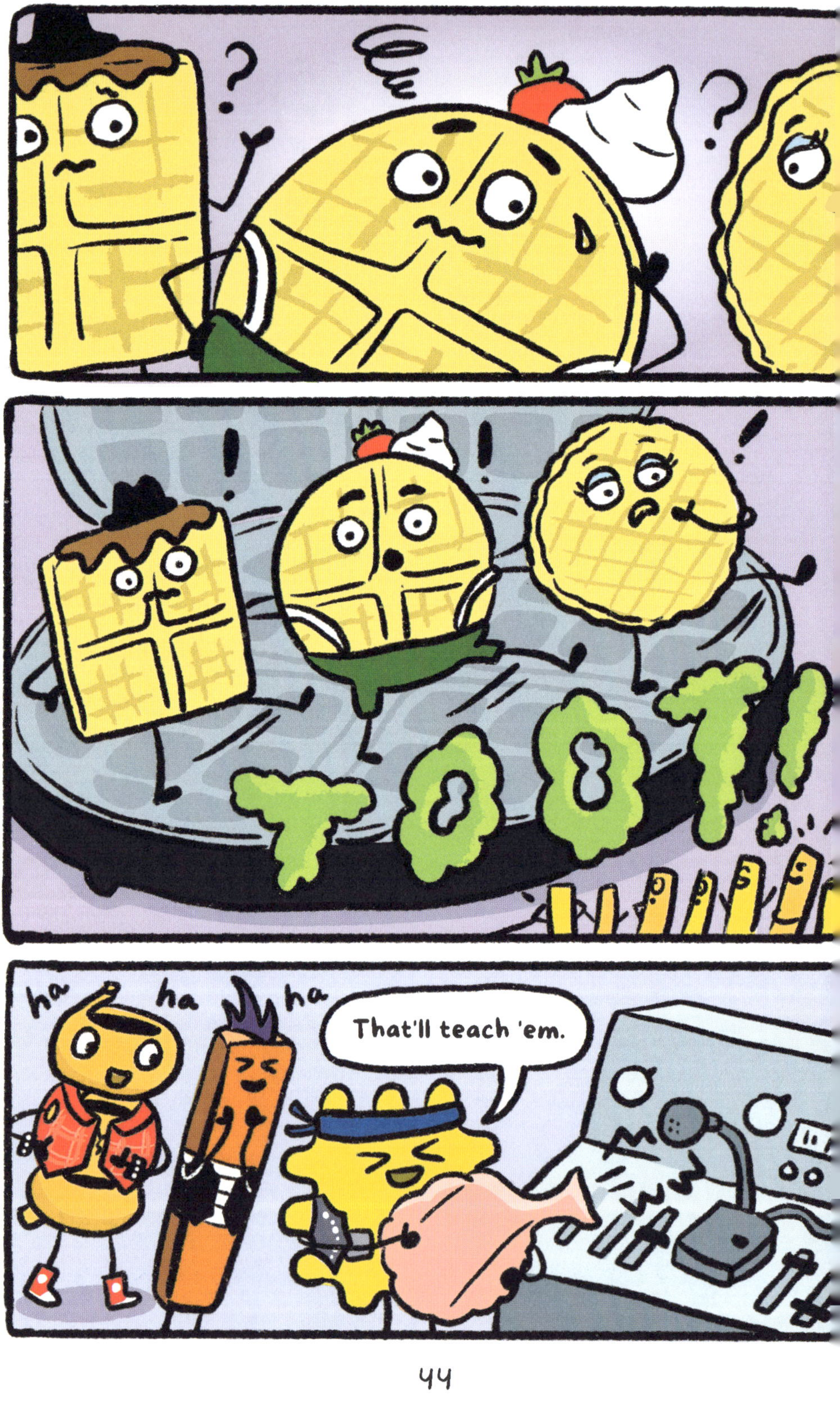
?
?
!
!
!
TOOT!!
ha
ha
ha
That'll teach 'em.

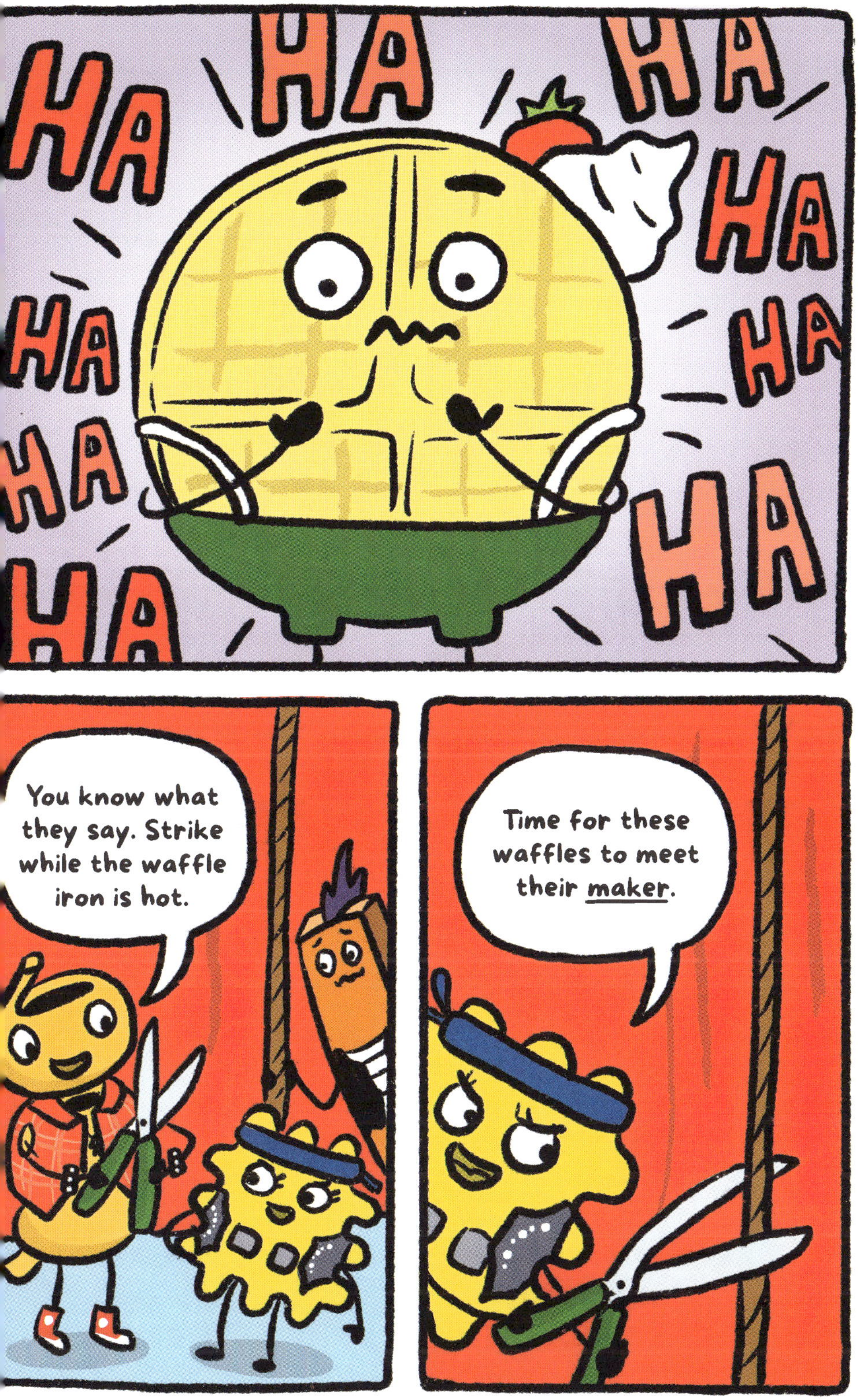
HA HA HA HA HA HA HA HA HA HA HA HA
You know what they say. Strike while the waffle iron is hot.
Time for these waffles to meet their maker.

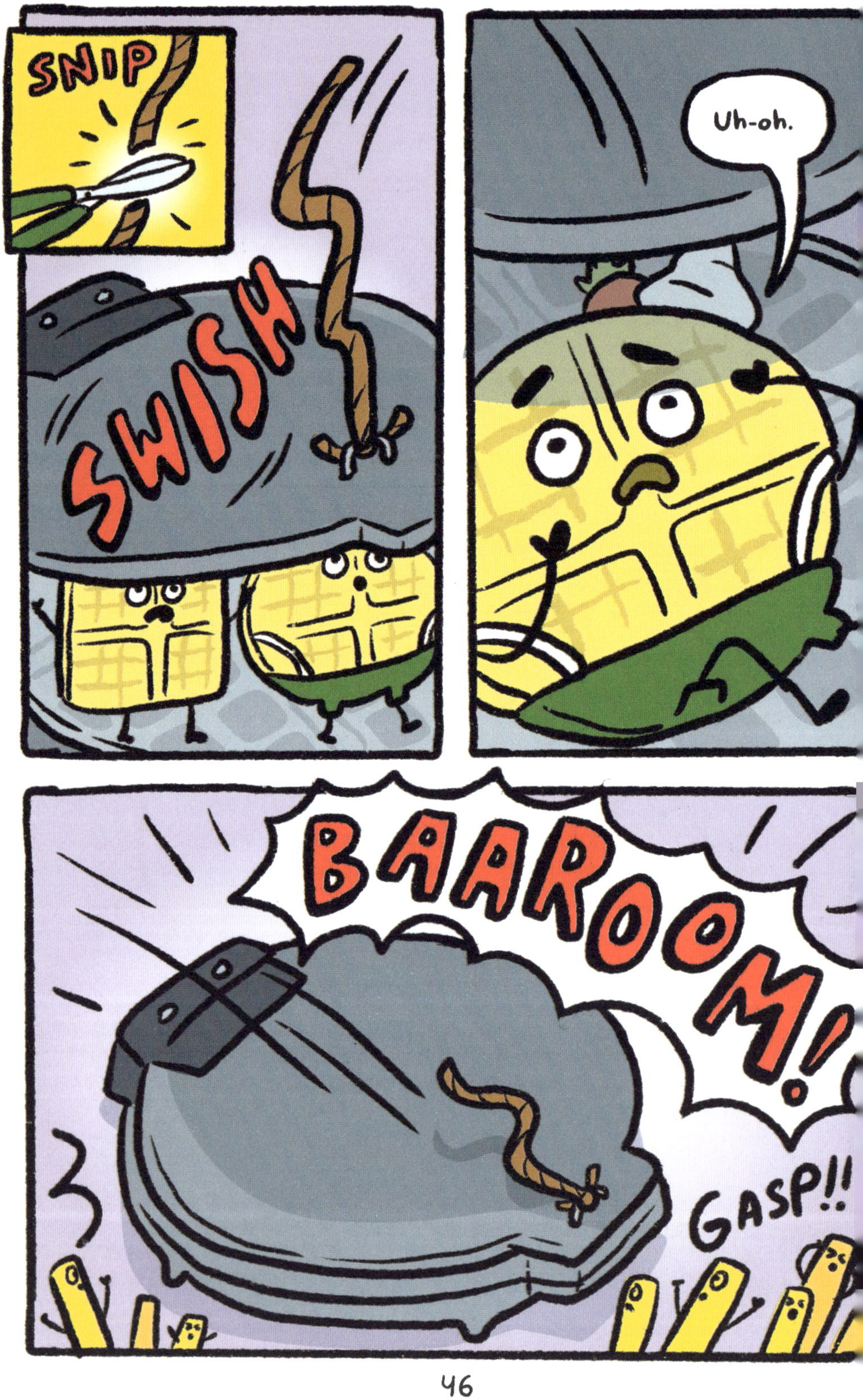
SNIP
SWISH
Uh-oh.
BAAROOM!
GASP!!

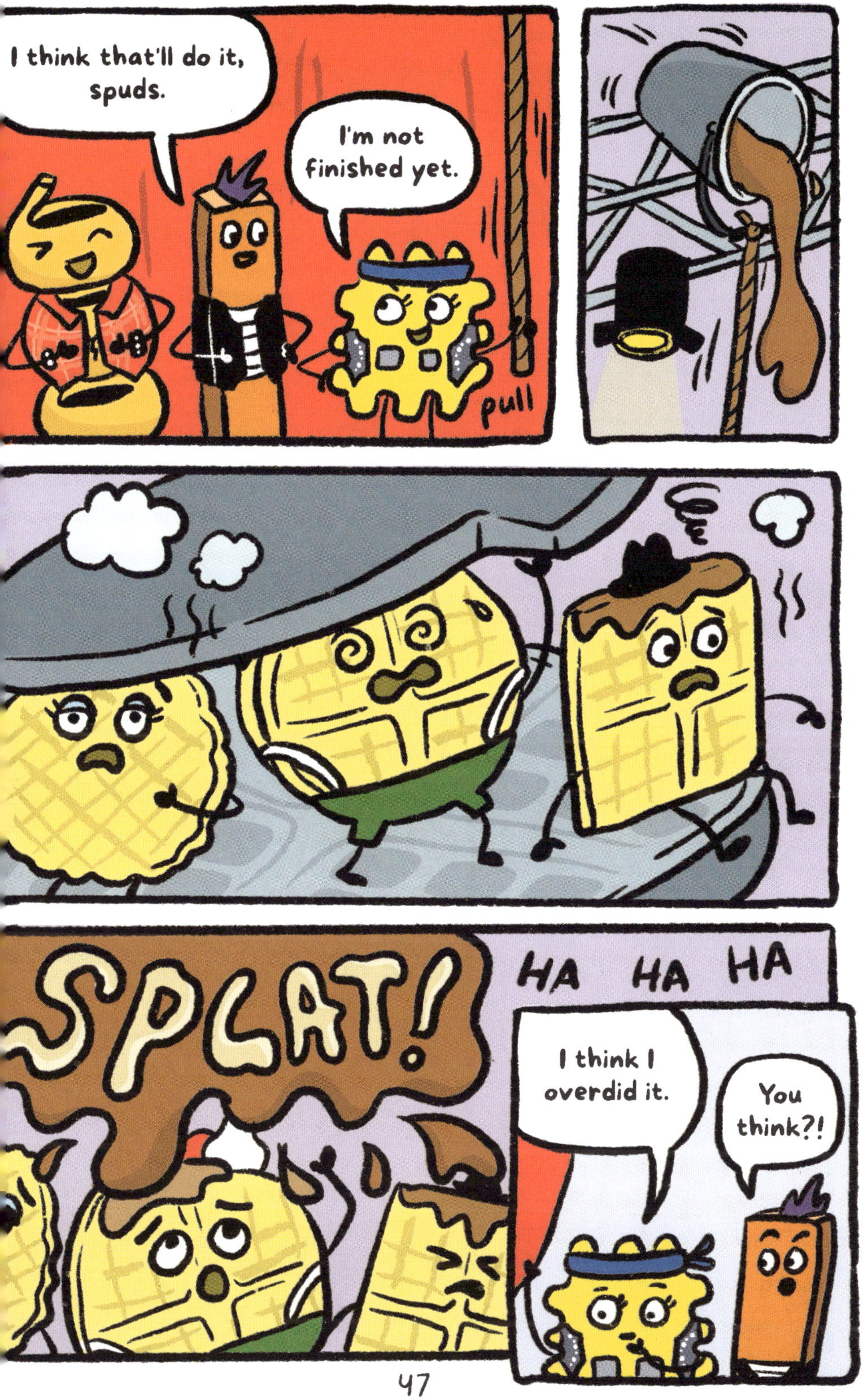
I think that'll do it, spuds.
I'm not finished yet.
pull
SPLAT!
HA HA HA
I think I overdid it.
You think?!

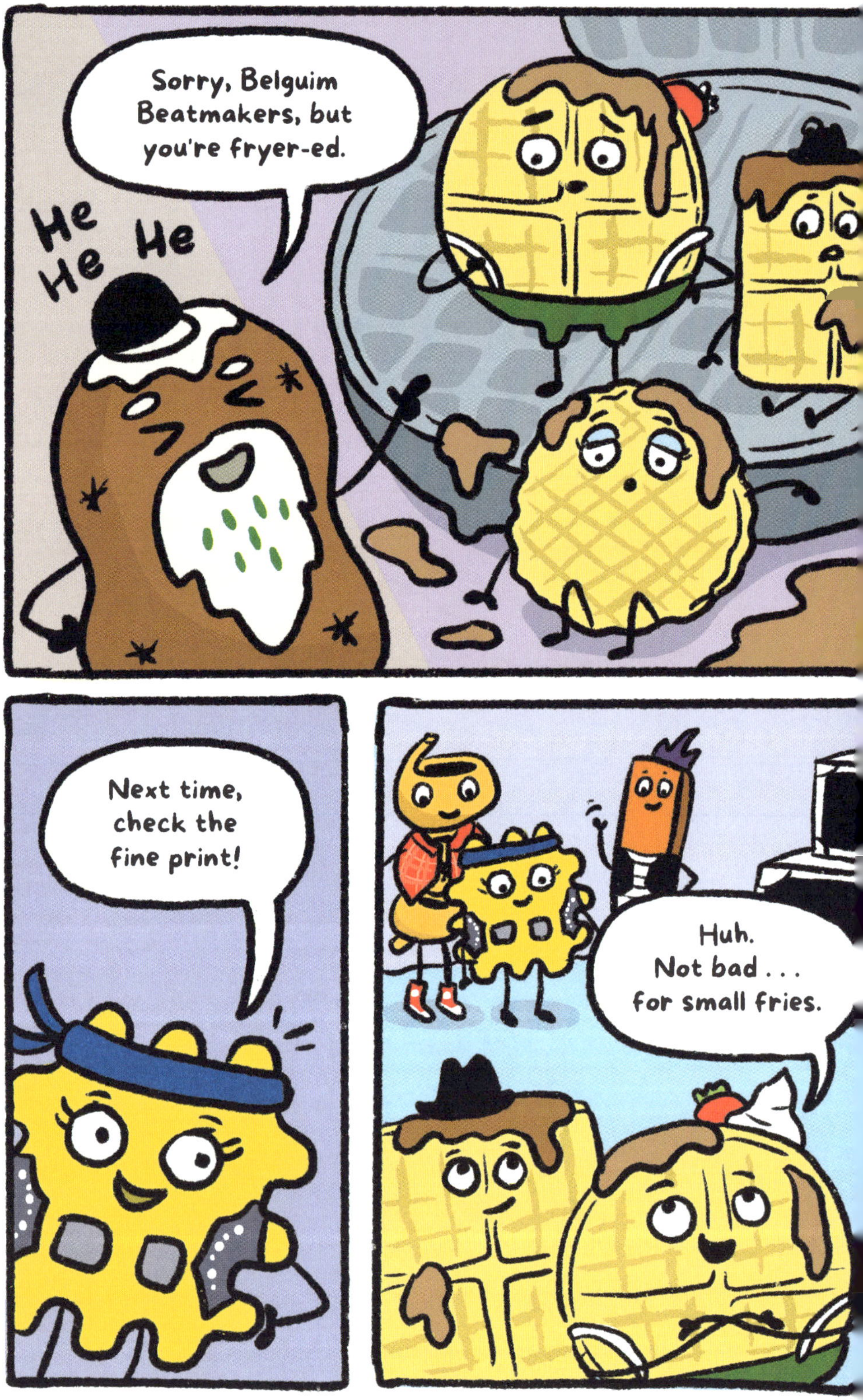
Sorry, Belguim Beatmakers, but you're fryer-ed.
He He He
Next time, check the fine print!
Huh. Not bad . . . for small fries.

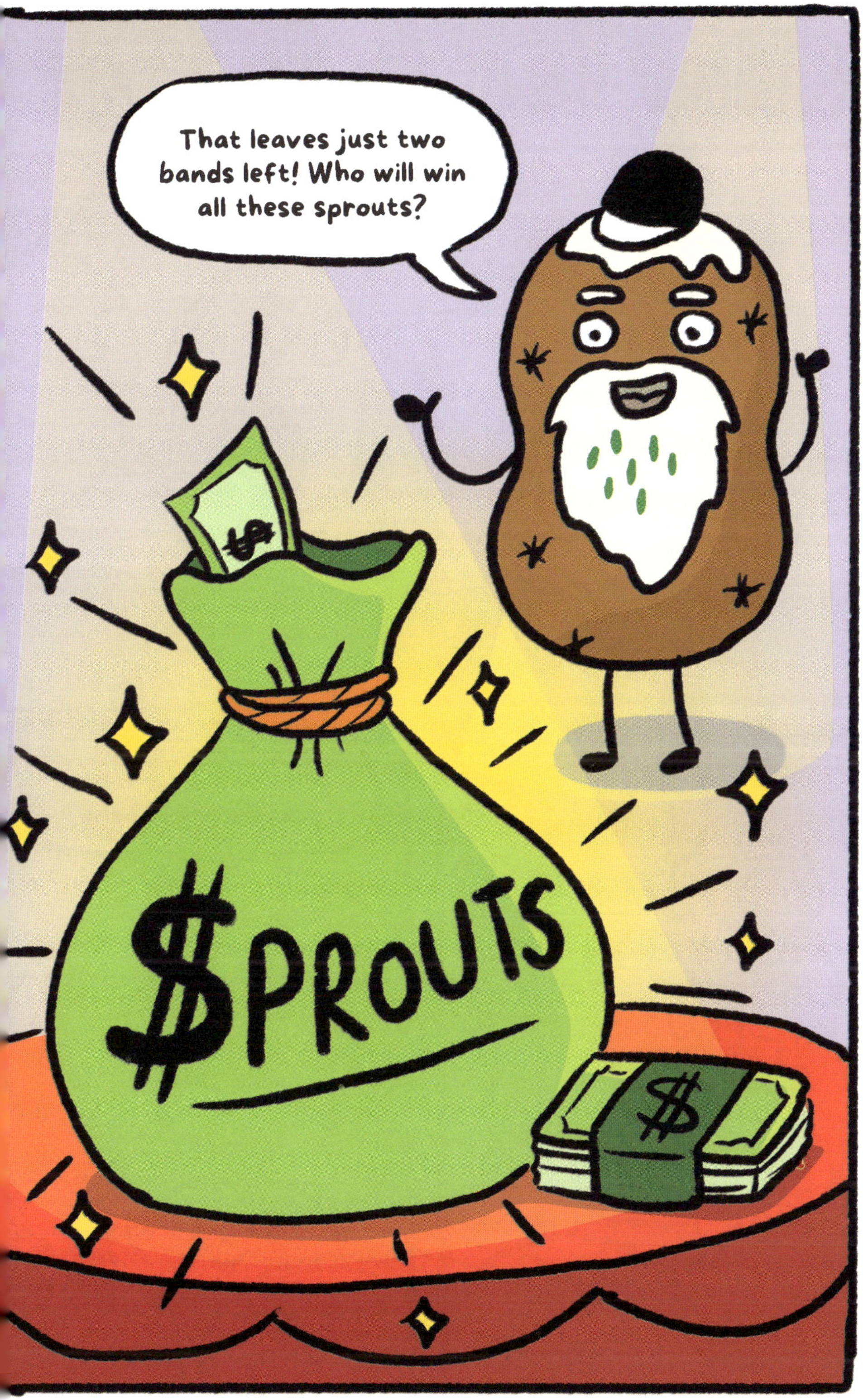
That leaves just two bands left! Who will win all these sprouts?
$PROUTS

CHAPTER 4 The Grand Fry-nale

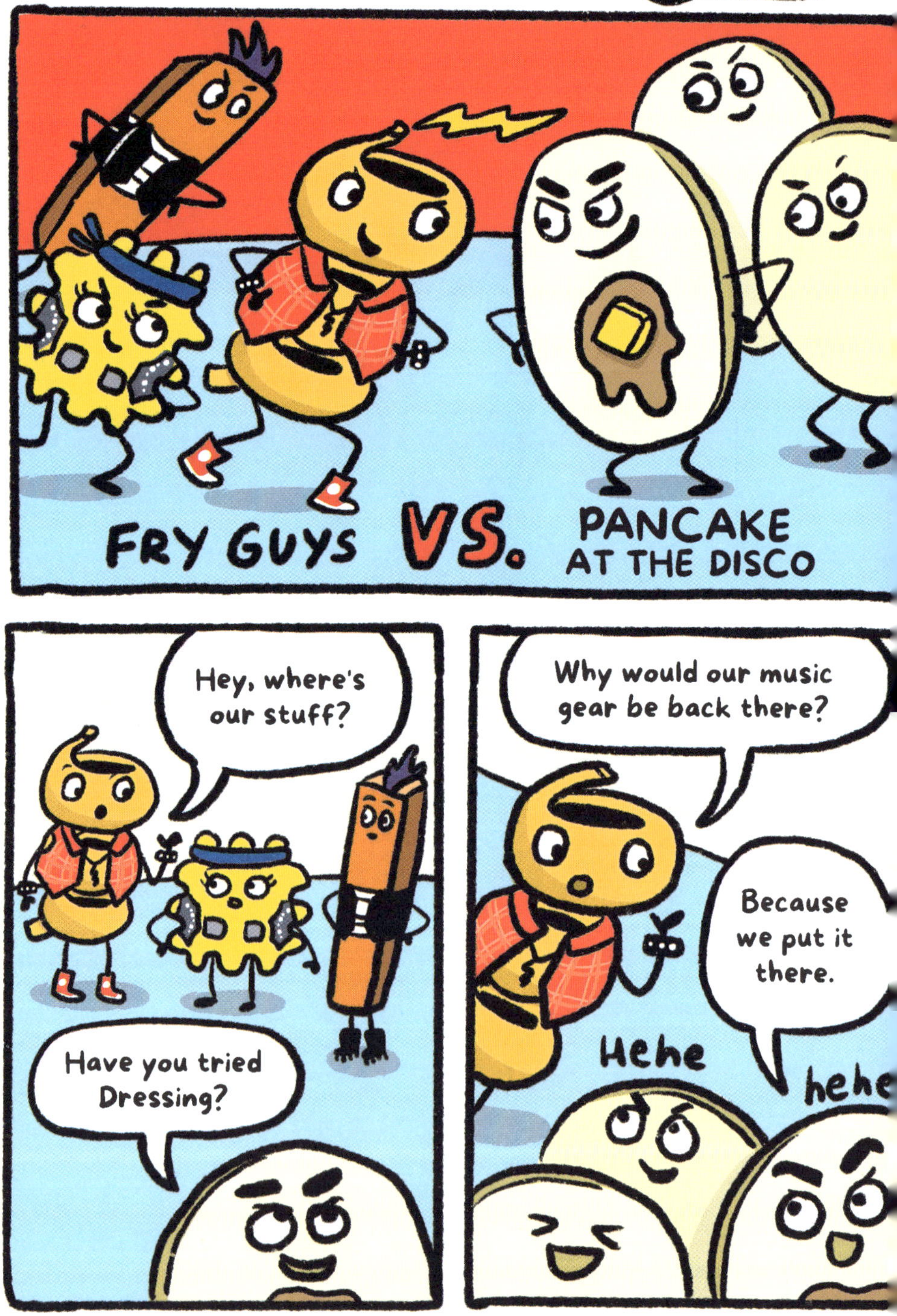

FRY GUYS VS. PANCAKE AT THE DISCO
Hey, where's our stuff?
Have you tried Dressing?
Why would our music gear be back there?
Because we put it there.
Hehe
hehe

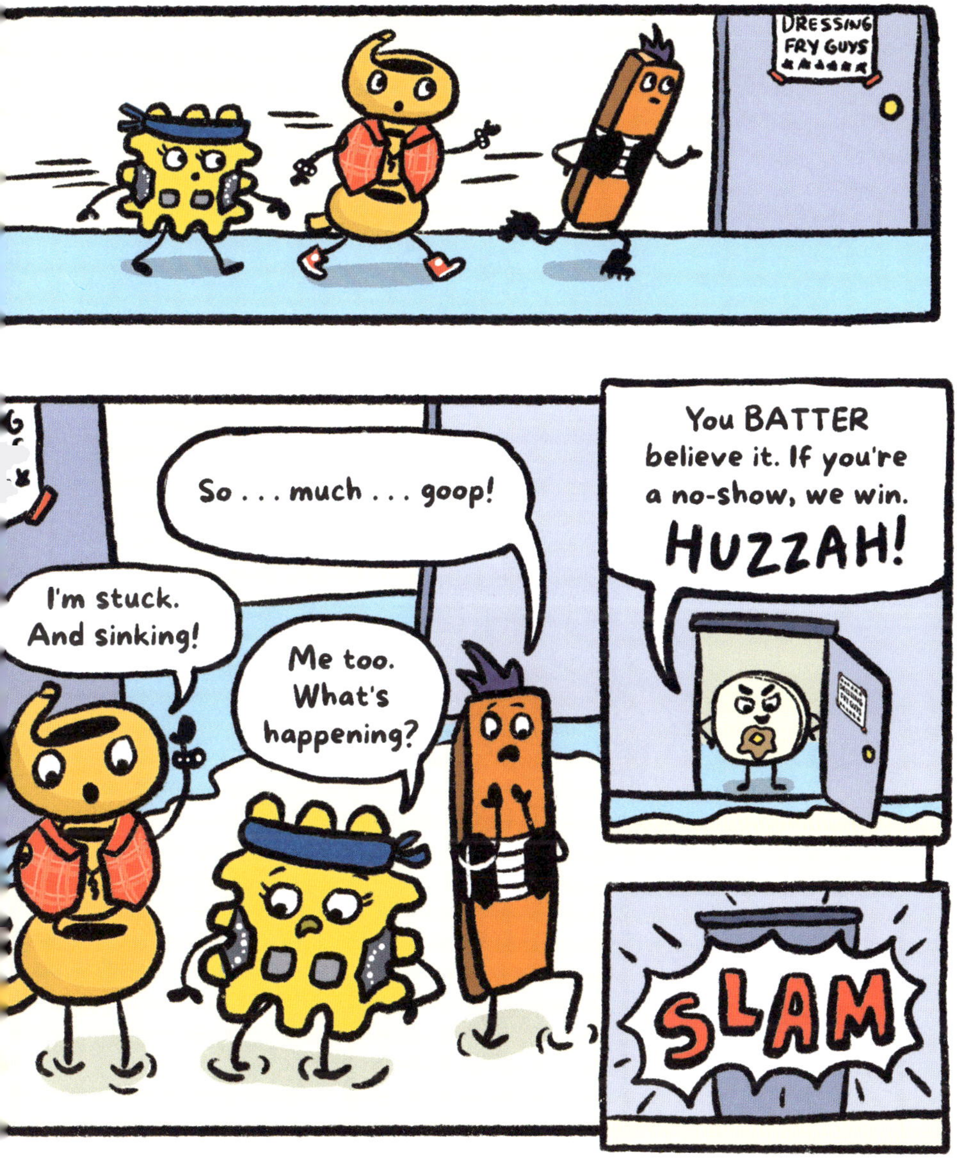
DRESSING
FRY GUYS
So . . . much . . . goop!
I'm stuck. And sinking!
Me too. What's happening?
You BATTER believe it. If you're a no-show, we win.
HUZZAH!
SLAM

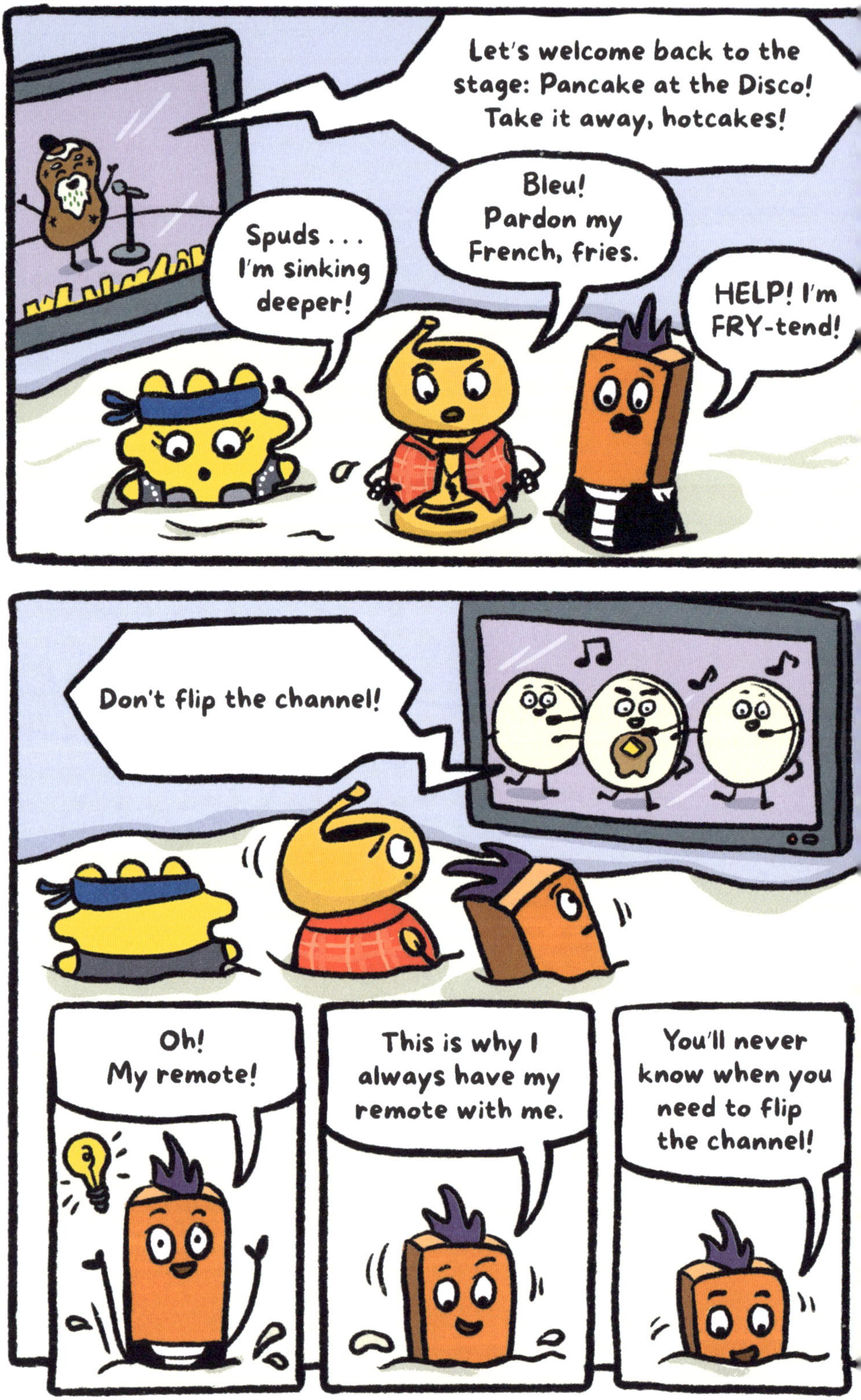
Let's welcome back to the stage: Pancake at the Disco! Take it away, hotcakes!
Spuds . . . I'm sinking deeper!
Bleu! Pardon my French, fries.
HELP! I'm FRY-tend!
Don't flip the channel!
Oh! My remote!
This is why I always have my remote with me.
You'll never know when you need to flip the channel!

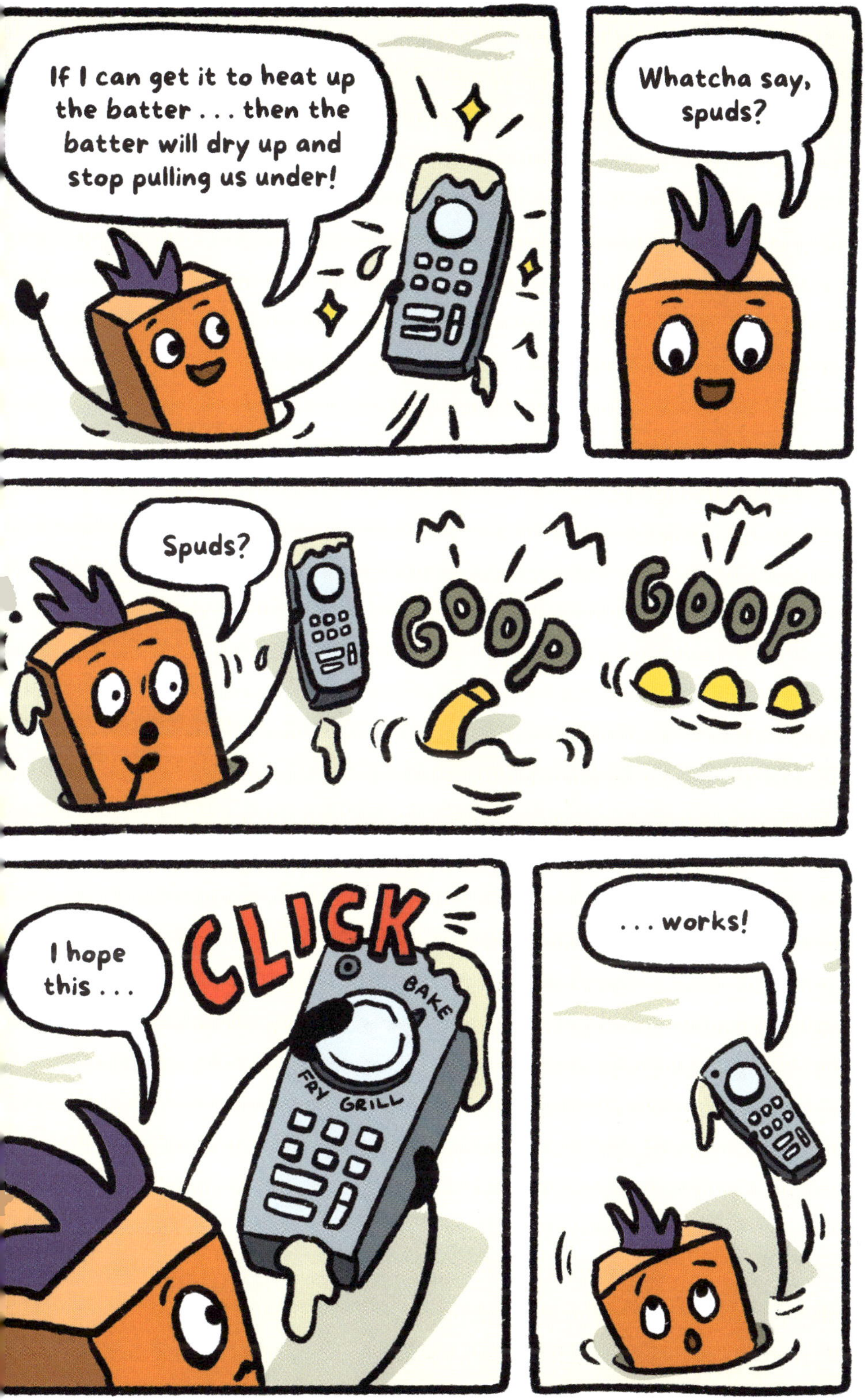
If I can get it to heat up the batter . . . then the batter will dry up and stop pulling us under!
Whatcha say, spuds?
Spuds?
GOOP
GOOP
I hope this . . .
CLICK
BAKE
FRY
GRILL
. . . works!

SQUELCH!

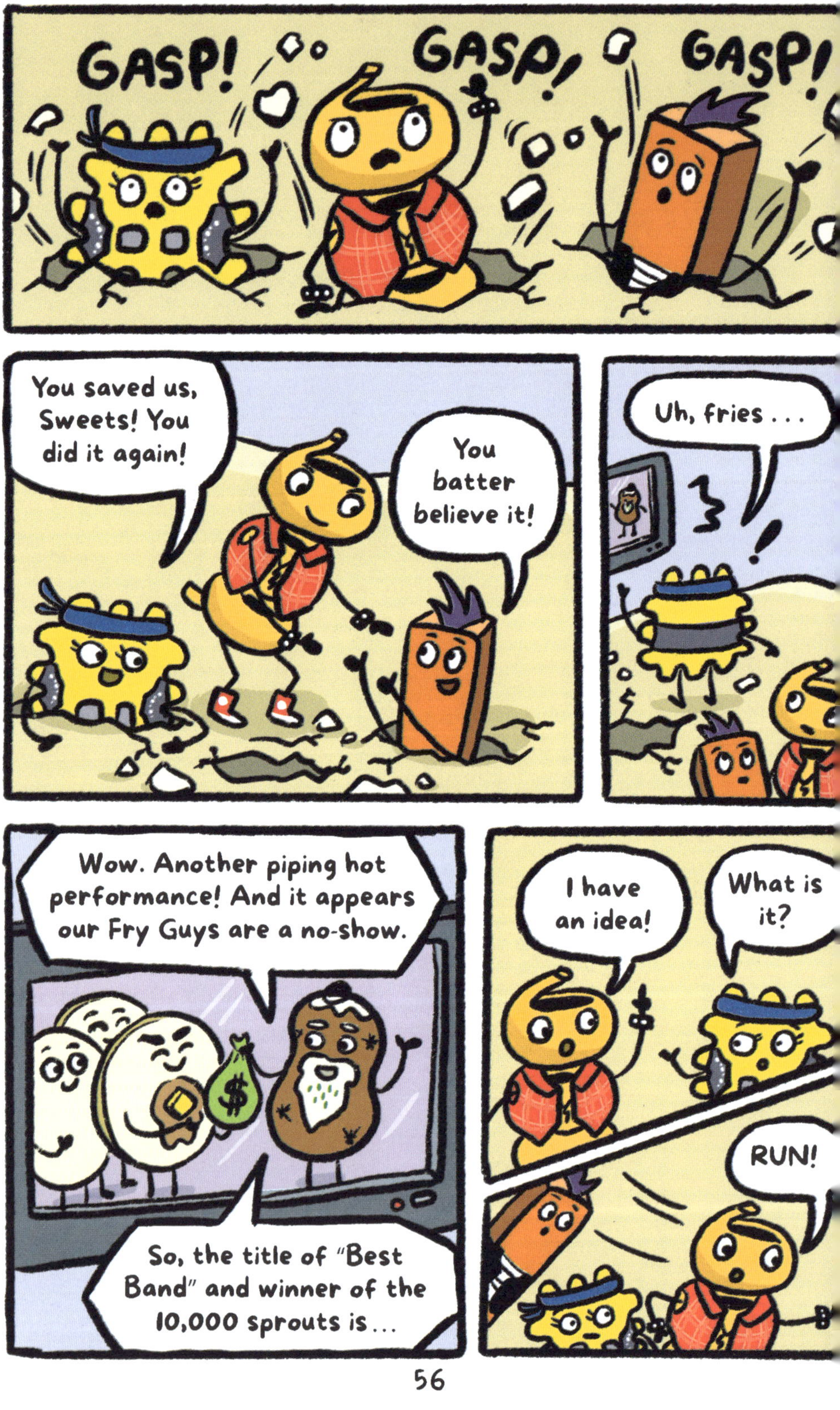
GASP!
GASP!
GASP!
You saved us, Sweets! You did it again!
You batter believe it!
Uh, fries . . .
Wow. Another piping hot performance! And it appears our Fry Guys are a no-show.
So, the title of "Best Band" and winner of the 10,000 sprouts is . . .
I have an idea!
What is it?
RUN!

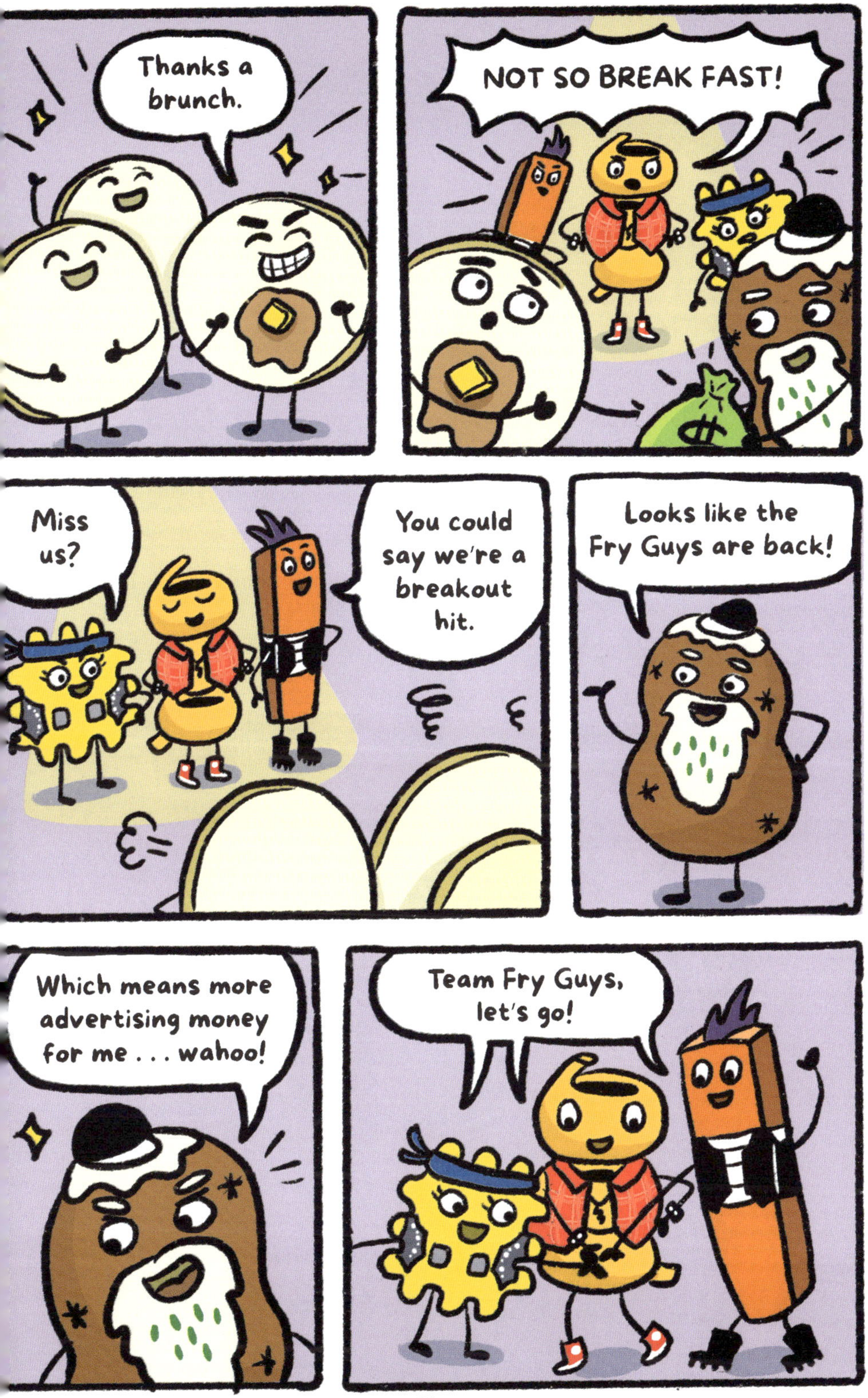
Thanks a brunch.
NOT SO BREAK FAST!
Miss us?
You could say we're a breakout hit.
Looks like the Fry Guys are back!
Which means more advertising money for me . . . wahoo!
Team Fry Guys, let's go!

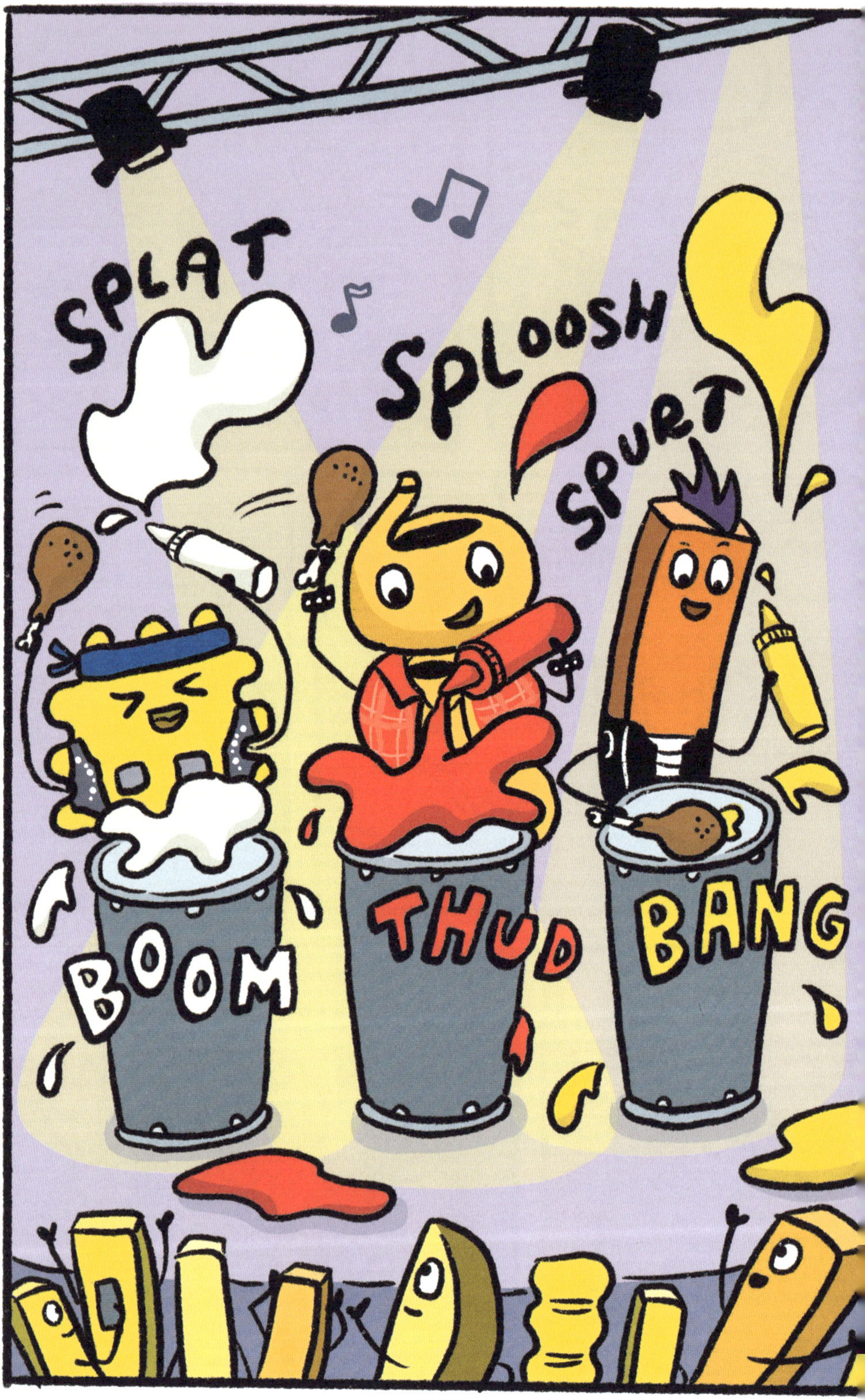
SPLAT
SPLOOSH
SPURT
BOOM
THUD
BANG

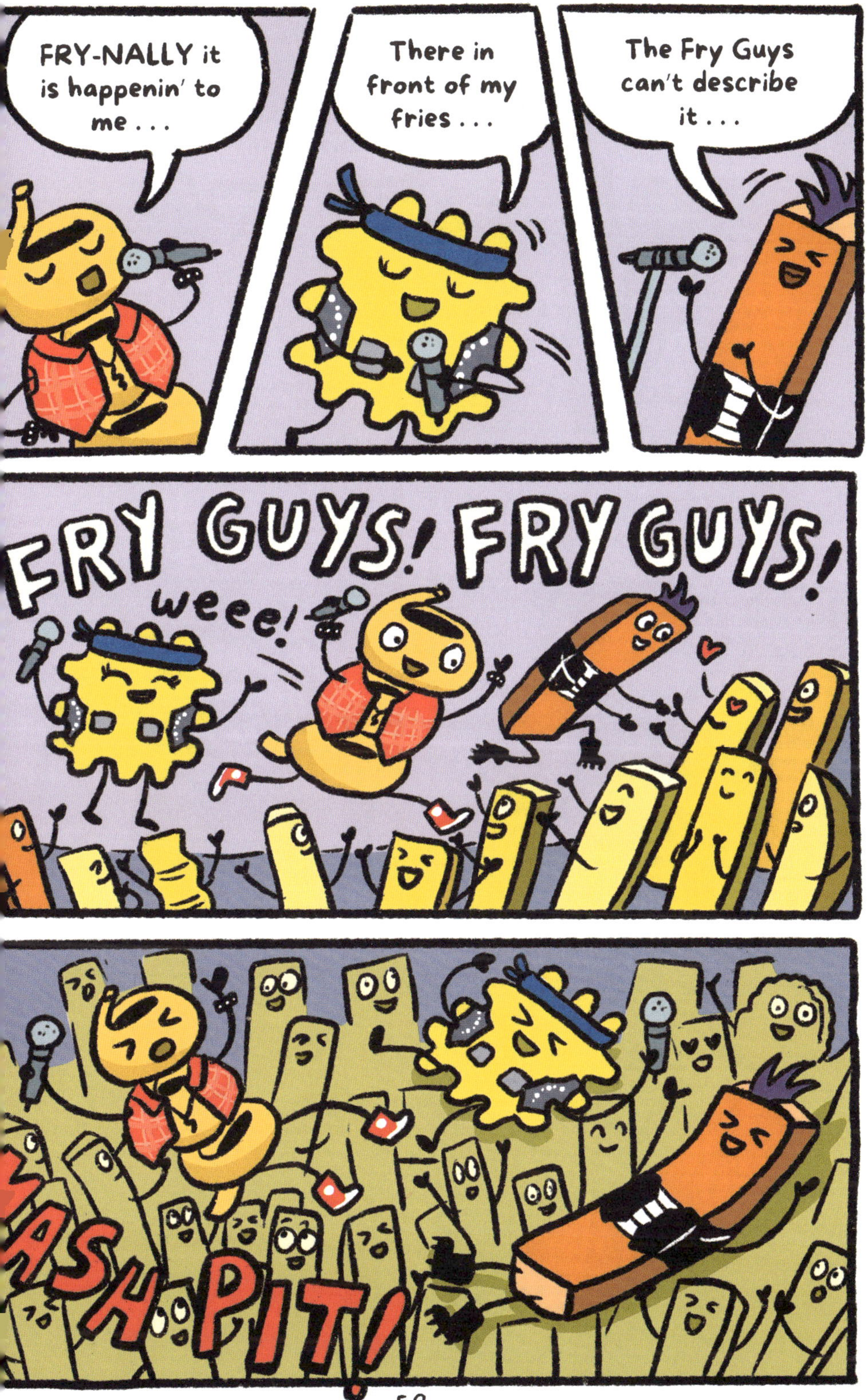

FRY-NALLY it is happenin' to me . . .
There in front of my fries . . .
The Fry Guys can't describe it . . .
FRY GUYS! FRY GUYS!
weeee!
MASH PIT!

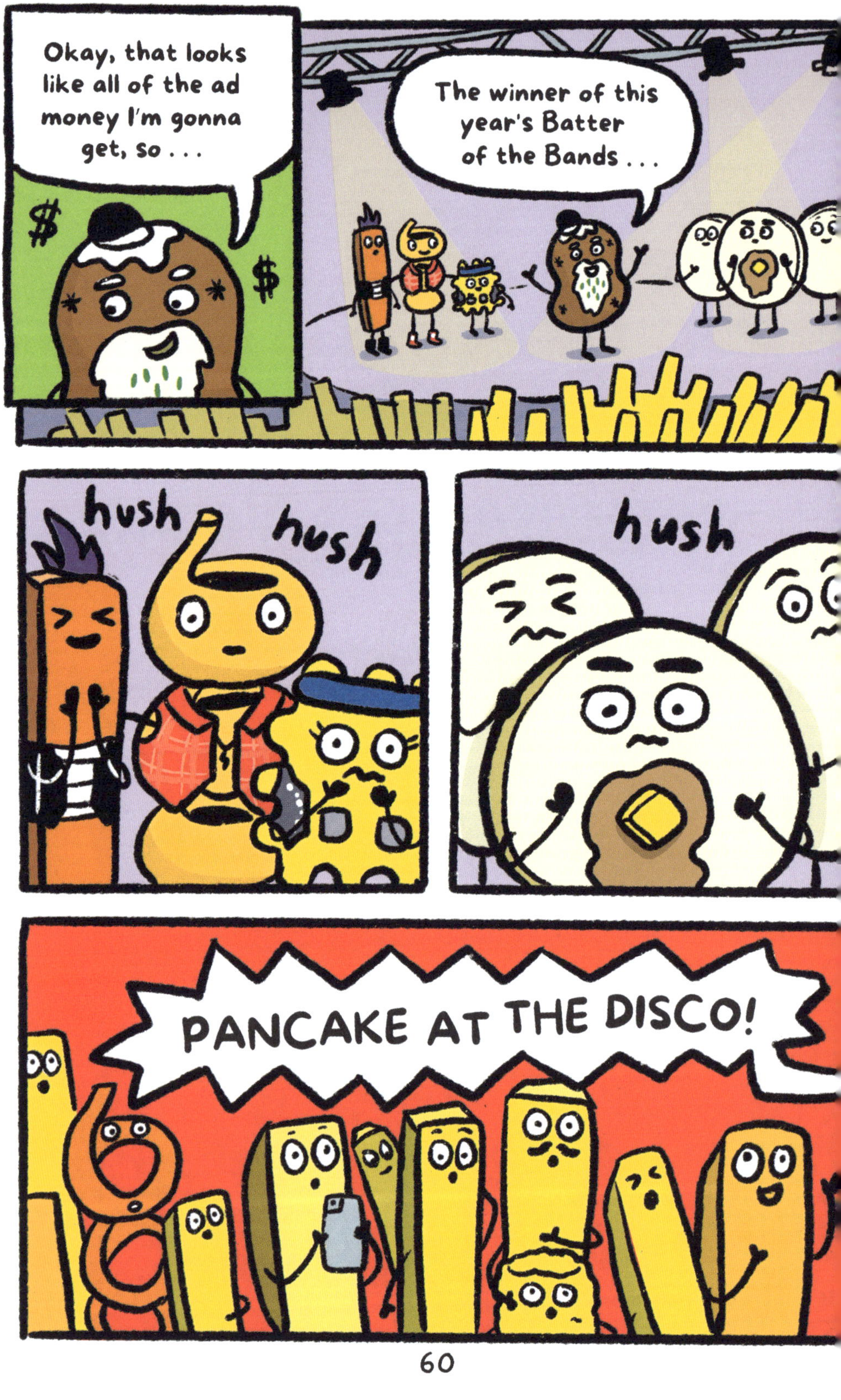
Okay, that looks like all of the ad money I'm gonna get, so . . .
The winner of this year's Batter of the Bands . . .
hush
hush
hush
PANCAKE AT THE DISCO!

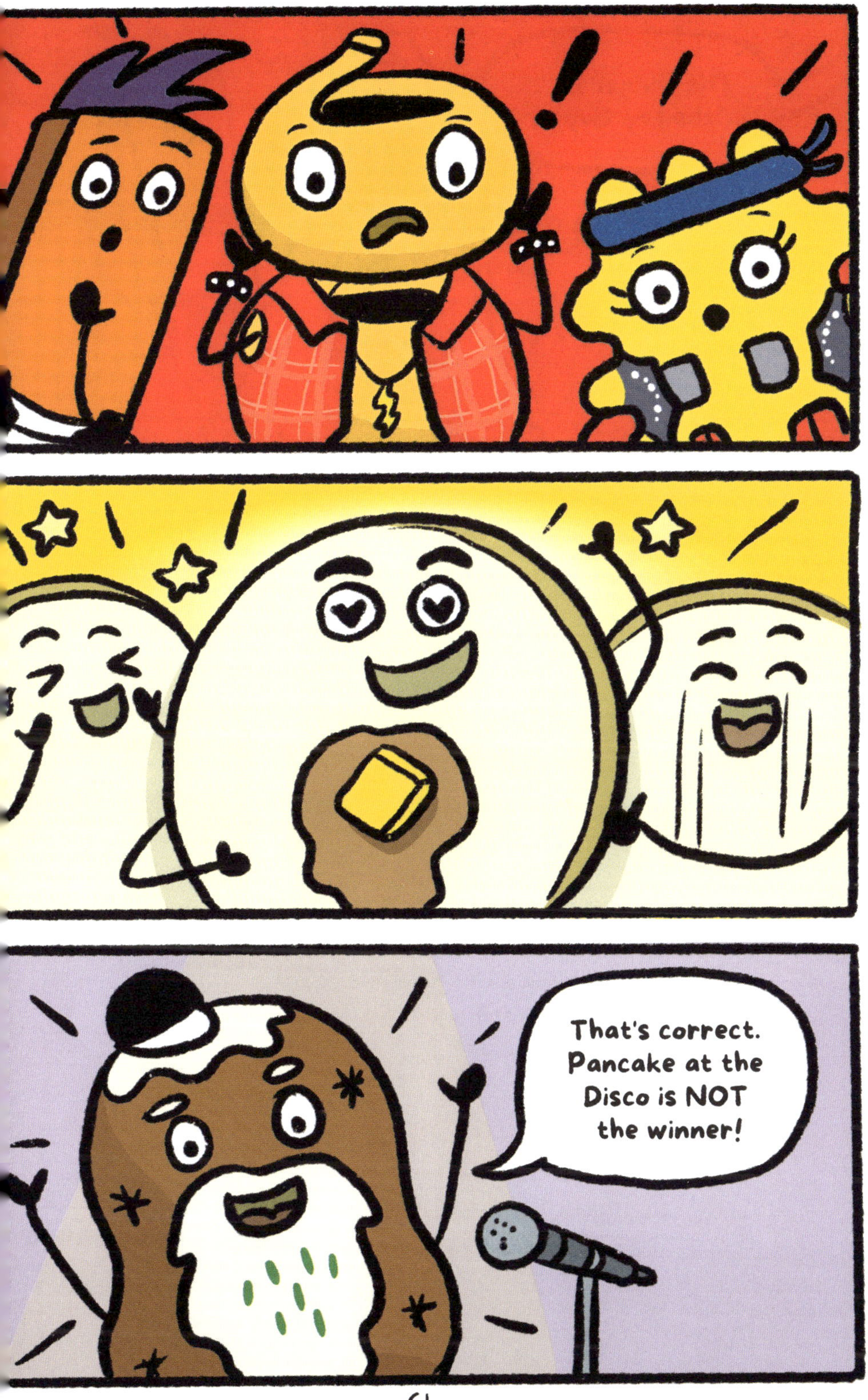
That's correct.
Pancake at the
Disco is NOT
the winner!

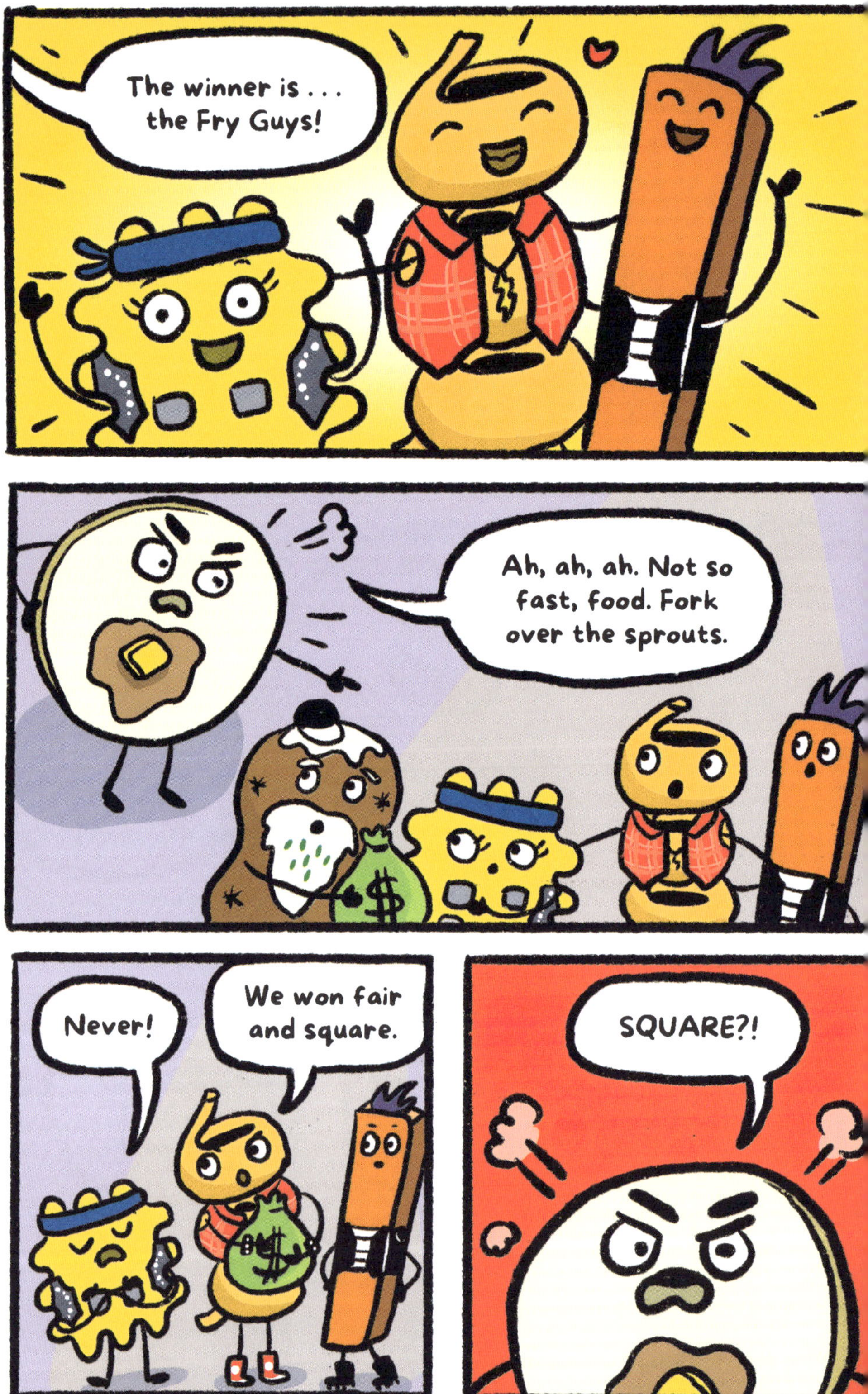
The winner is . . . the Fry Guys!
Ah, ah, ah. Not so fast, food. Fork over the sprouts.
Never!
We won fair and square.
SQUARE?!

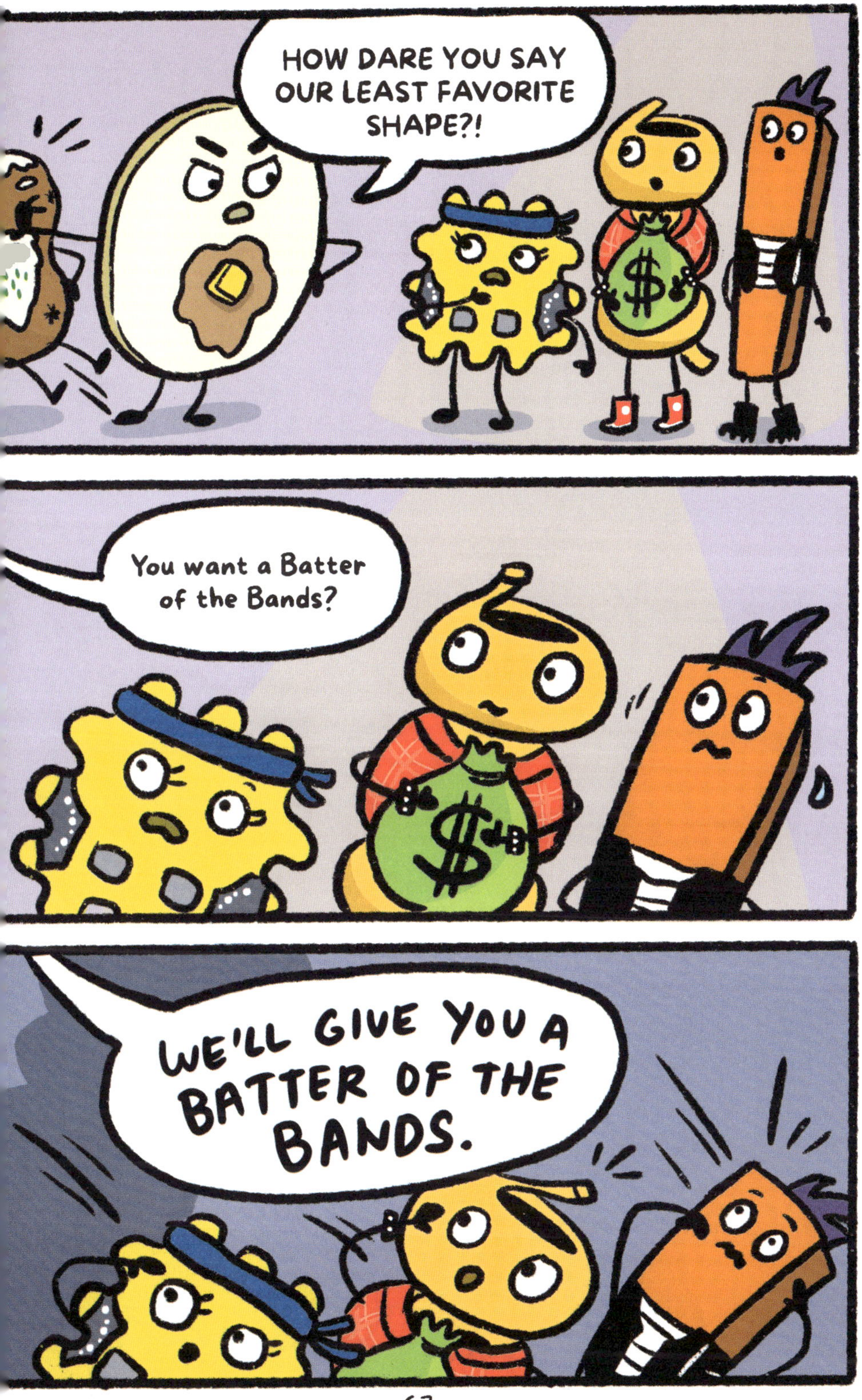
HOW DARE YOU SAY OUR LEAST FAVORITE SHAPE?!
You want a Batter of the Bands?
WE'LL GIVE YOU A BATTER OF THE BANDS.

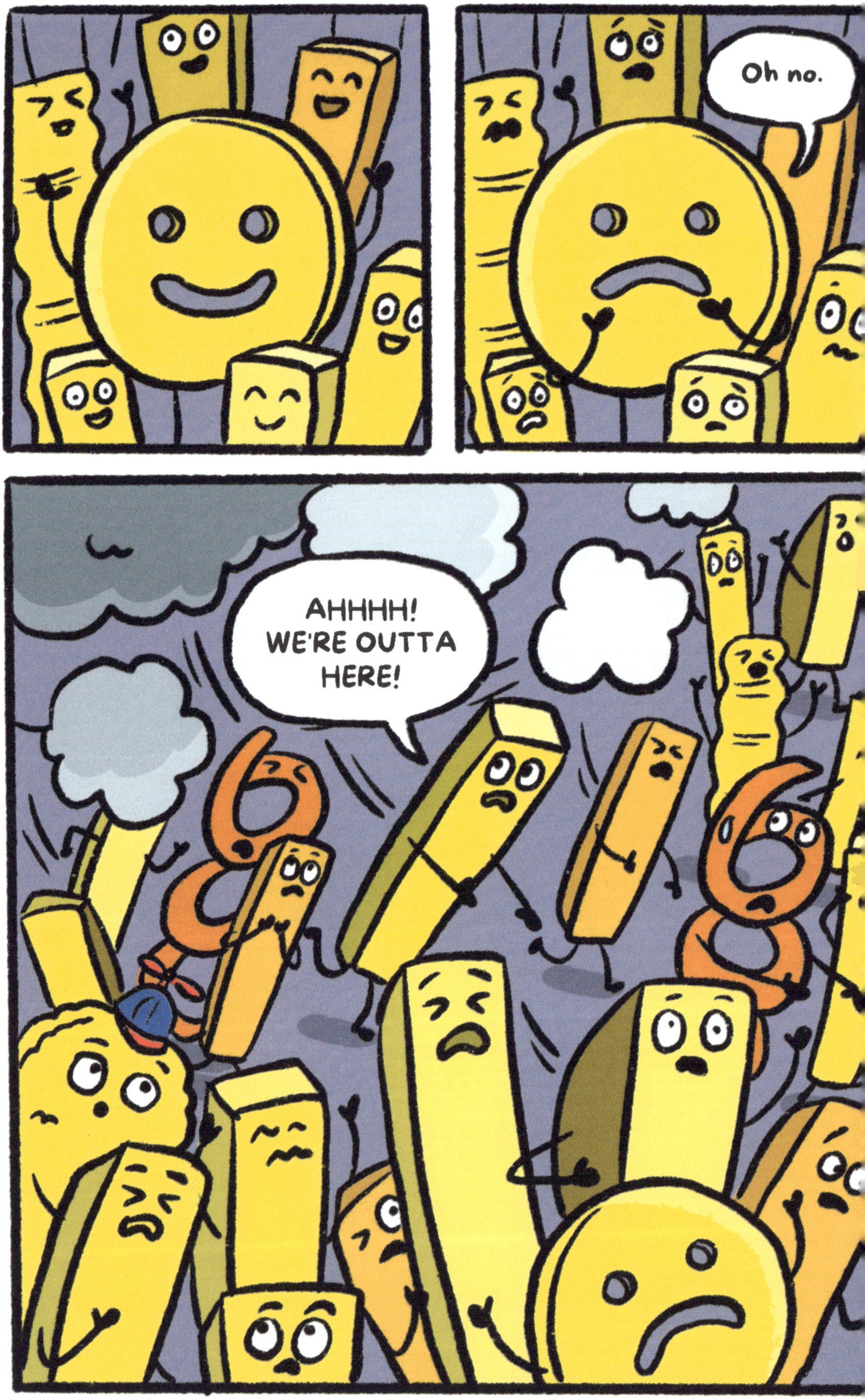
Oh no.
AHHHH! WE'RE OUTTA HERE!

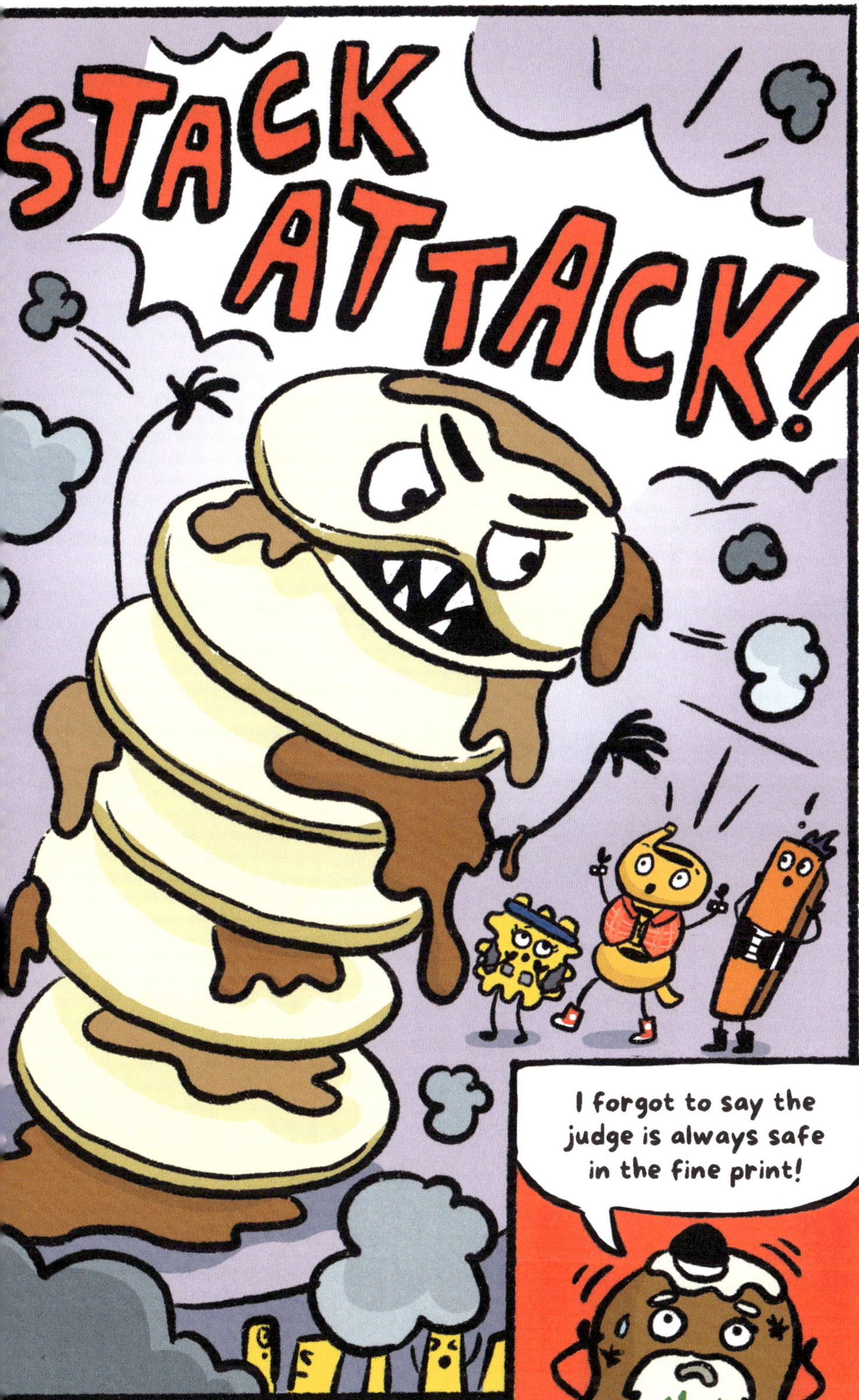
STACK ATTACK!
I forgot to say the judge is always safe in the fine print!

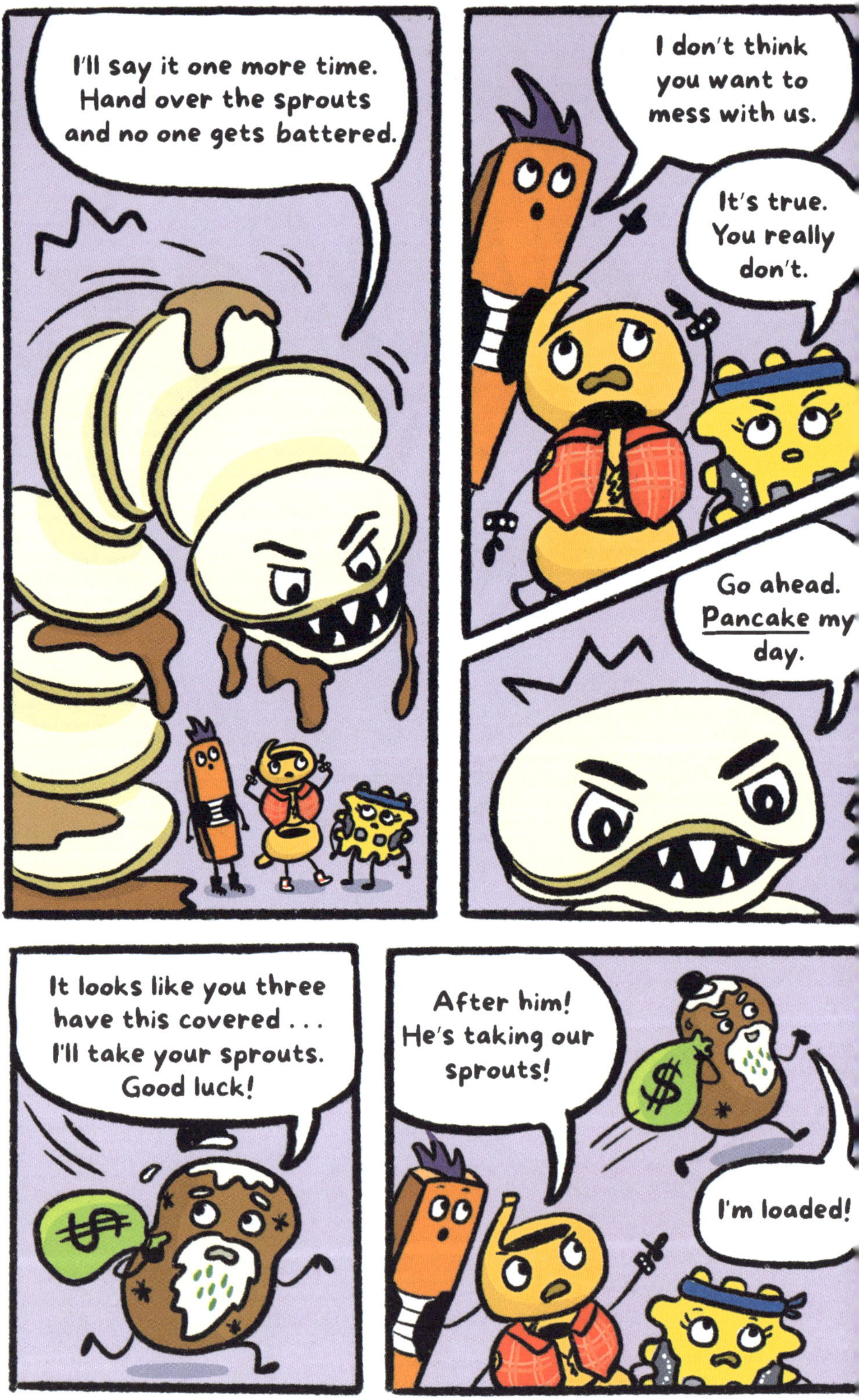
I'll say it one more time. Hand over the sprouts and no one gets battered.
I don't think you want to mess with us.
It's true. You really don't.
Go ahead. Pancake my day.
It looks like you three have this covered . . . I'll take your sprouts. Good luck!
After him! He's taking our sprouts!
I'm loaded!

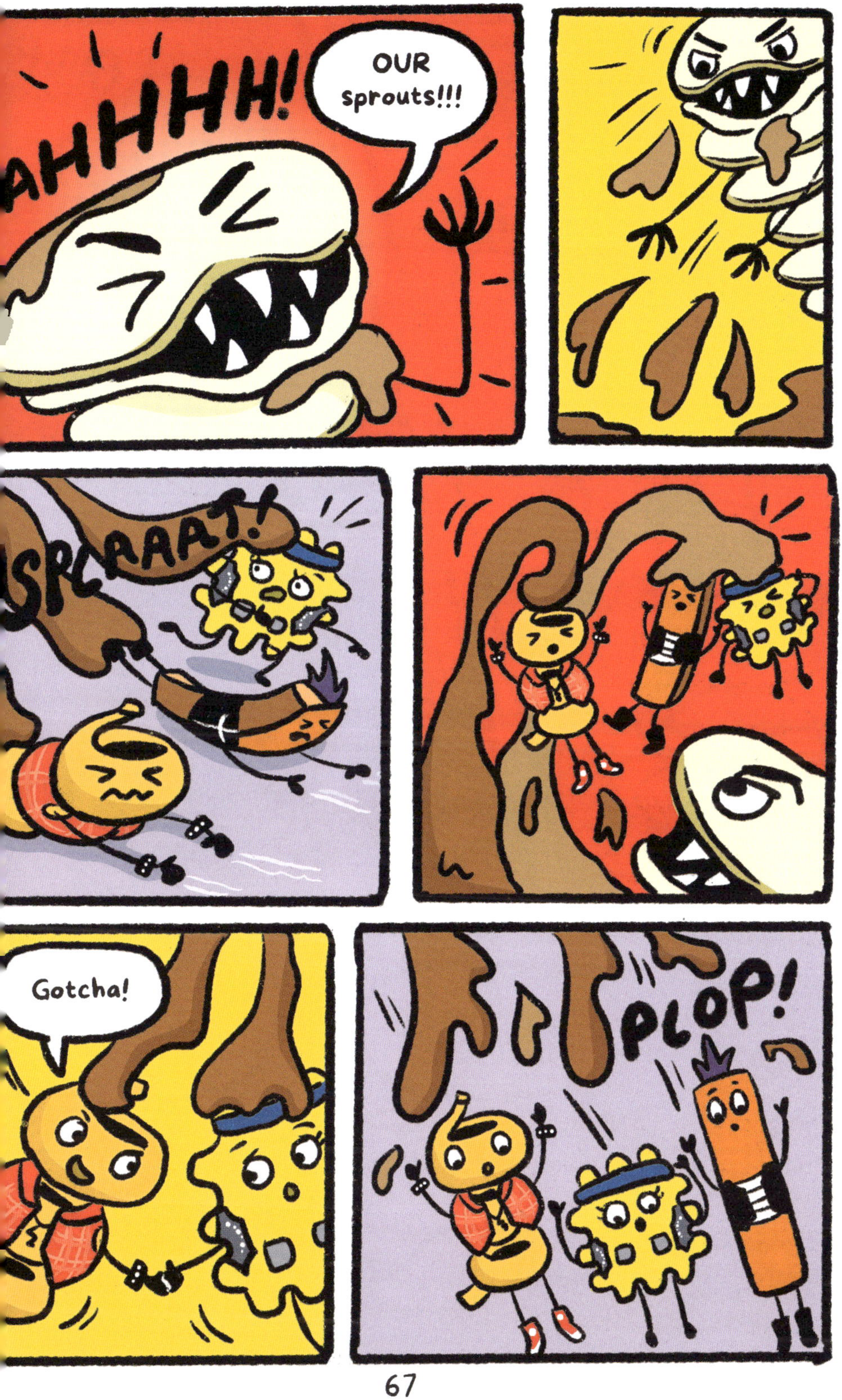
AHHHH!
OUR sprouts!!!
SPLRAAT!
Gotcha!
PLOP!

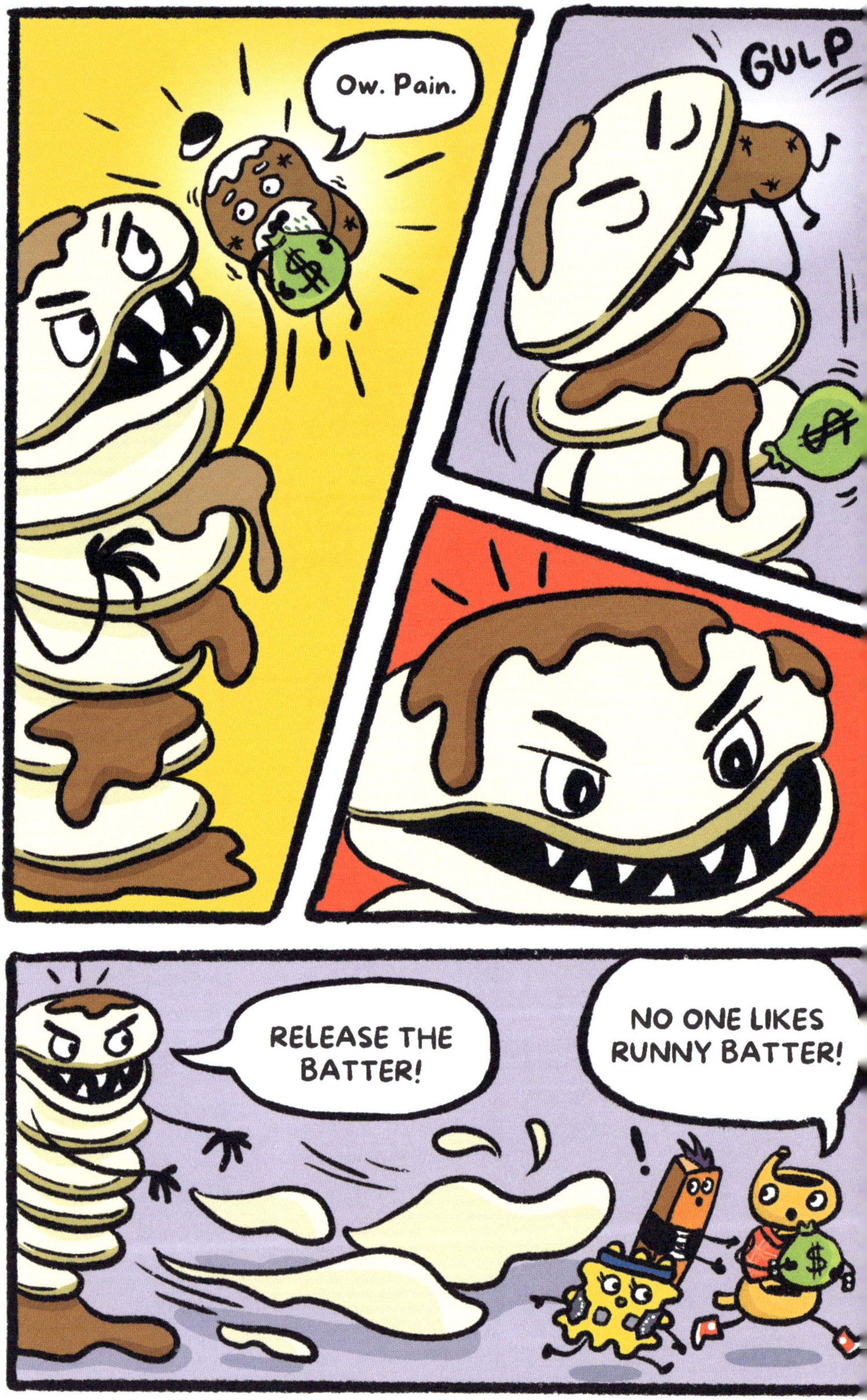
Ow. Pain.
GULP
RELEASE THE BATTER!
NO ONE LIKES RUNNY BATTER!

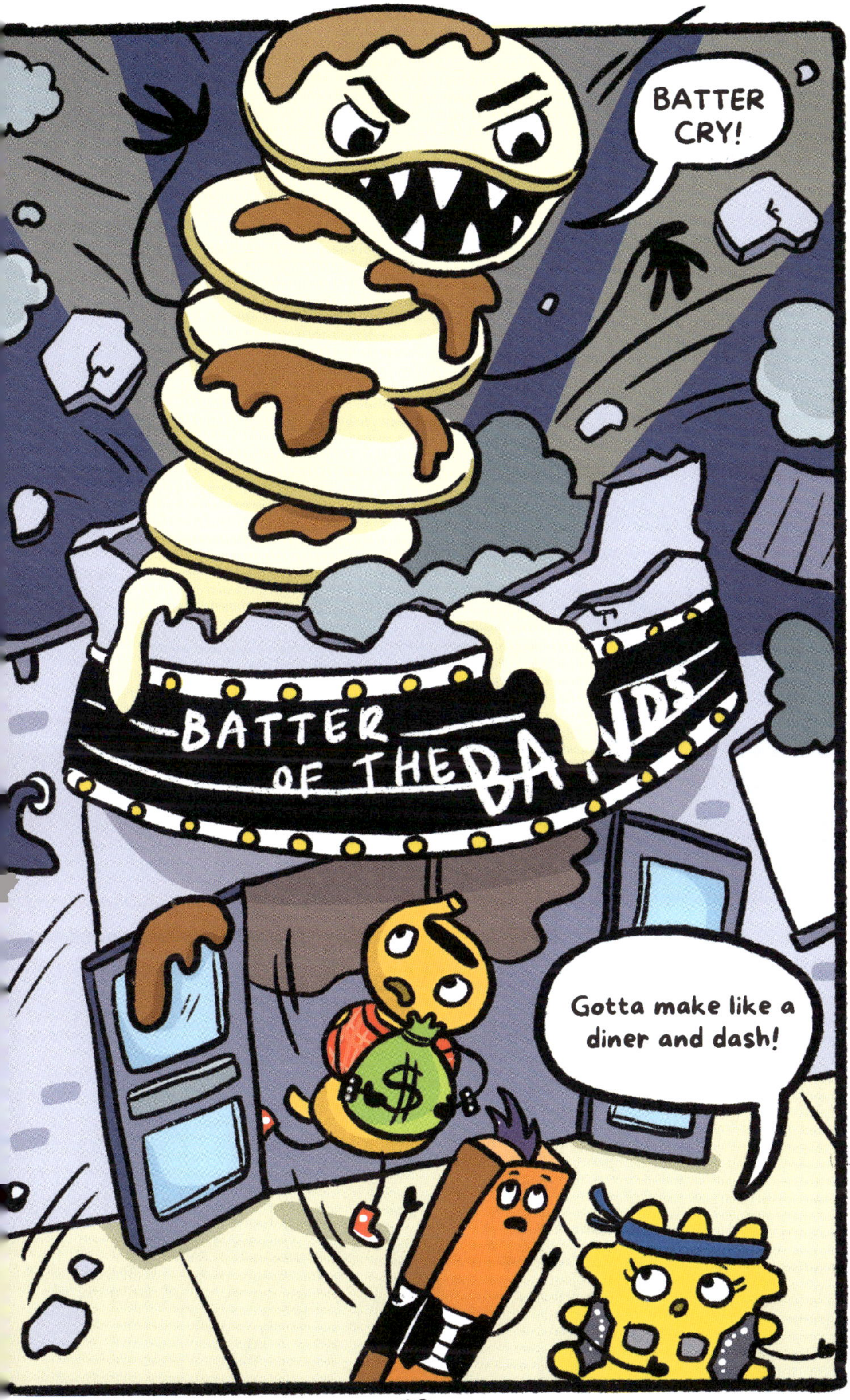
BATTER CRY!
BATTER OF THE BANDS
Gotta make like a diner and dash!

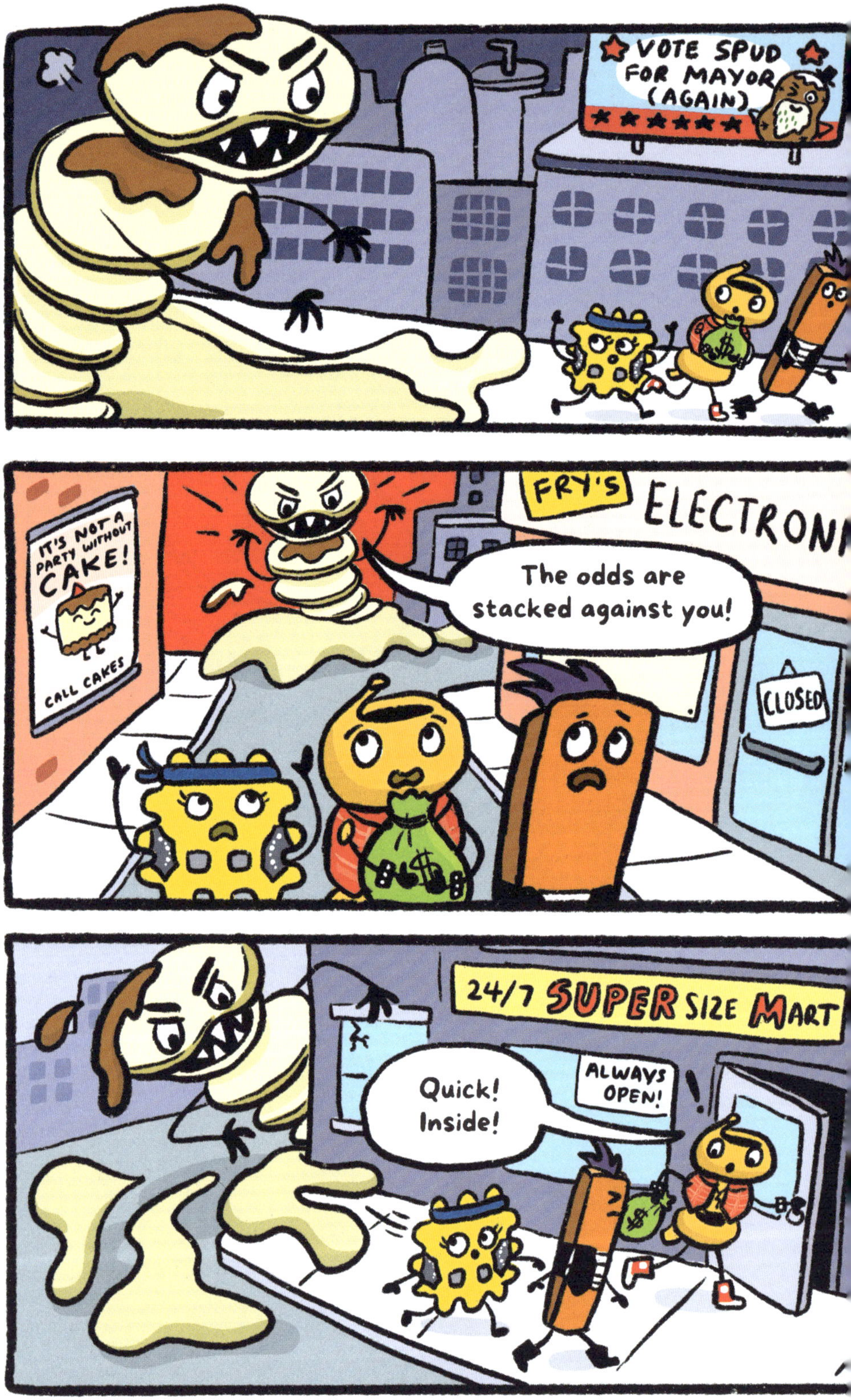
VOTE SPUD FOR MAYOR (AGAIN)
IT'S NOT A PARTY WITHOUT CAKE!
CALL CAKES
FRY'S ELECTRON
The odds are stacked against you!
CLOSED
24/7 SUPER SIZE MART
ALWAYS OPEN!
Quick! Inside!

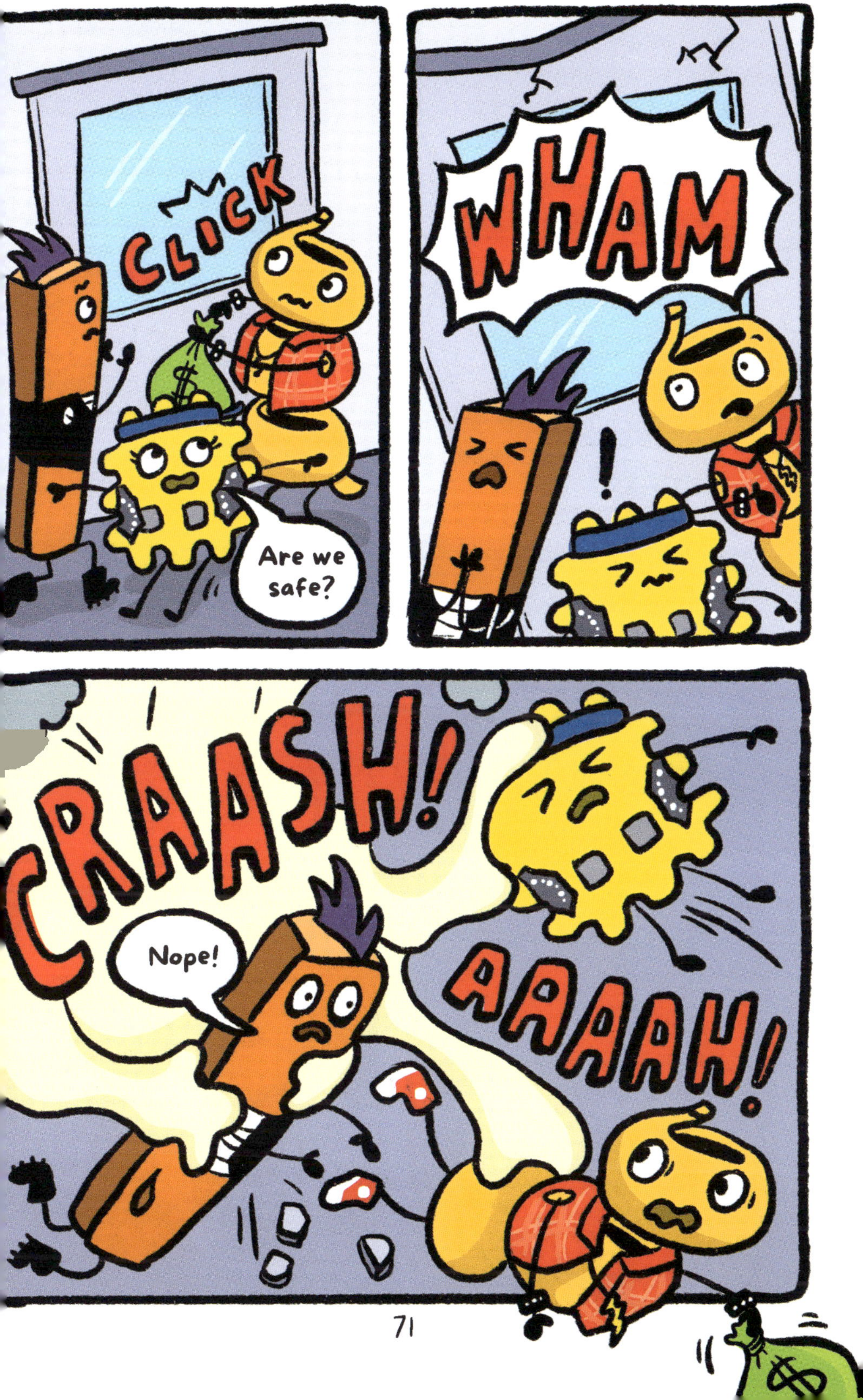
CLICK
Are we safe?
WHAM
!
CRAASH!
Nope!
AAAAAH!

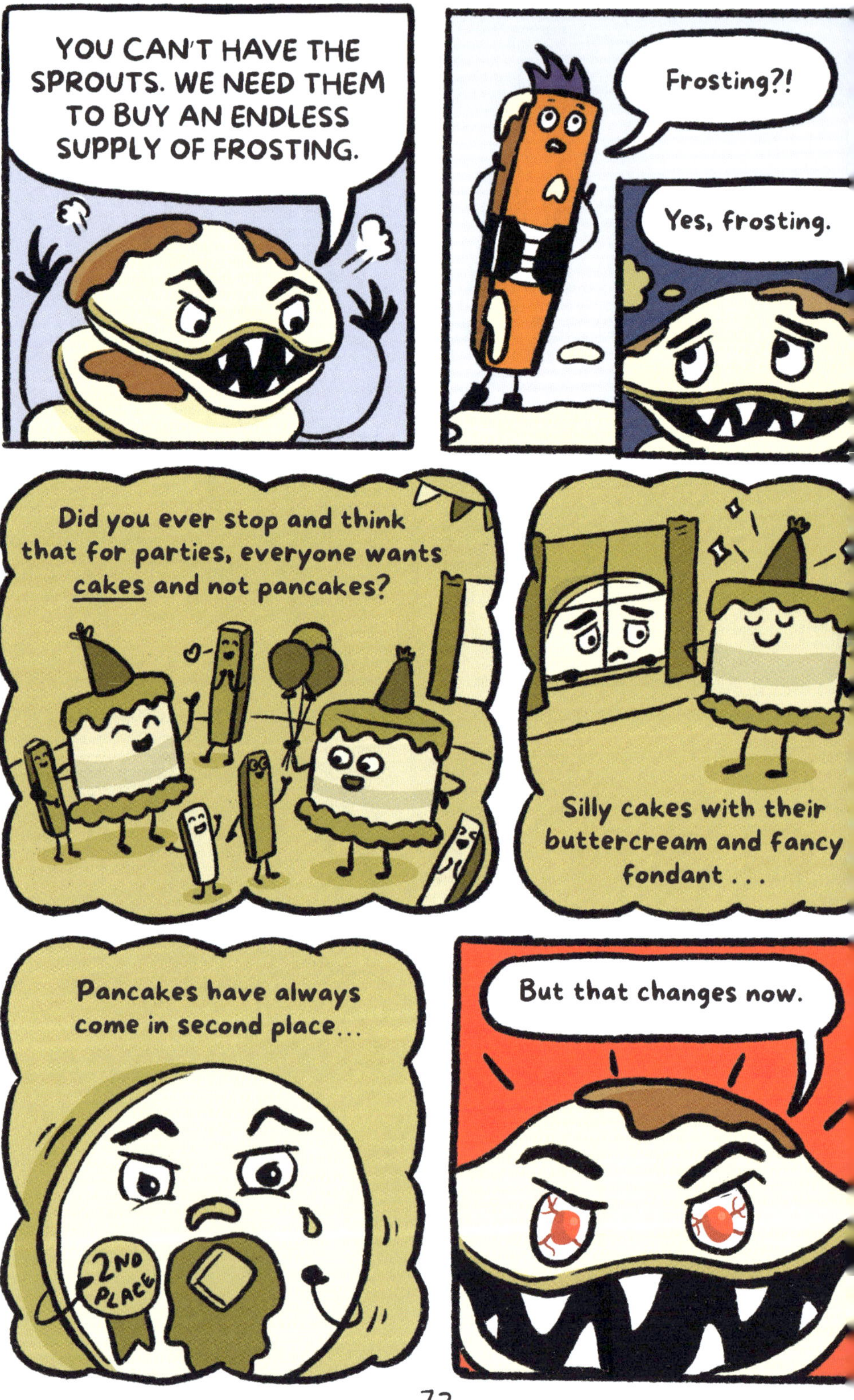
YOU CAN'T HAVE THE SPROUTS. WE NEED THEM TO BUY AN ENDLESS SUPPLY OF FROSTING.
Frosting?!
Yes, frosting.
Did you ever stop and think that for parties, everyone wants cakes and not pancakes?
Silly cakes with their buttercream and fancy fondant . . .
Pancakes have always come in second place...
2ND PLACE
But that changes now.

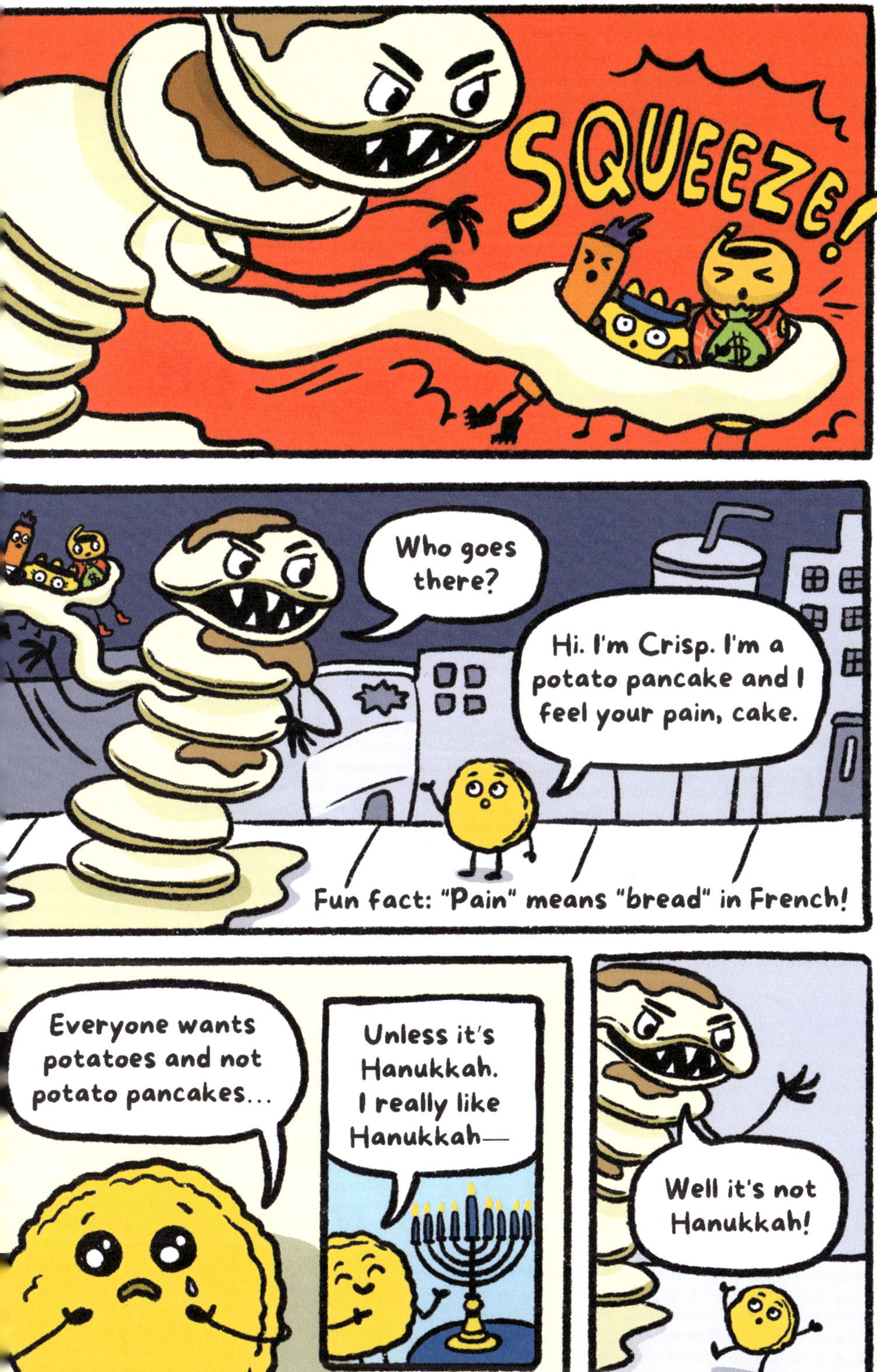
SQUEEZE!
Who goes there?
Hi. I'm Crisp. I'm a potato pancake and I feel your pain, cake.
Fun fact: "Pain" means "bread" in French!
Everyone wants potatoes and not potato pancakes...
Unless it's Hanukkah. I really like Hanukkah—
Well it's not Hanukkah!

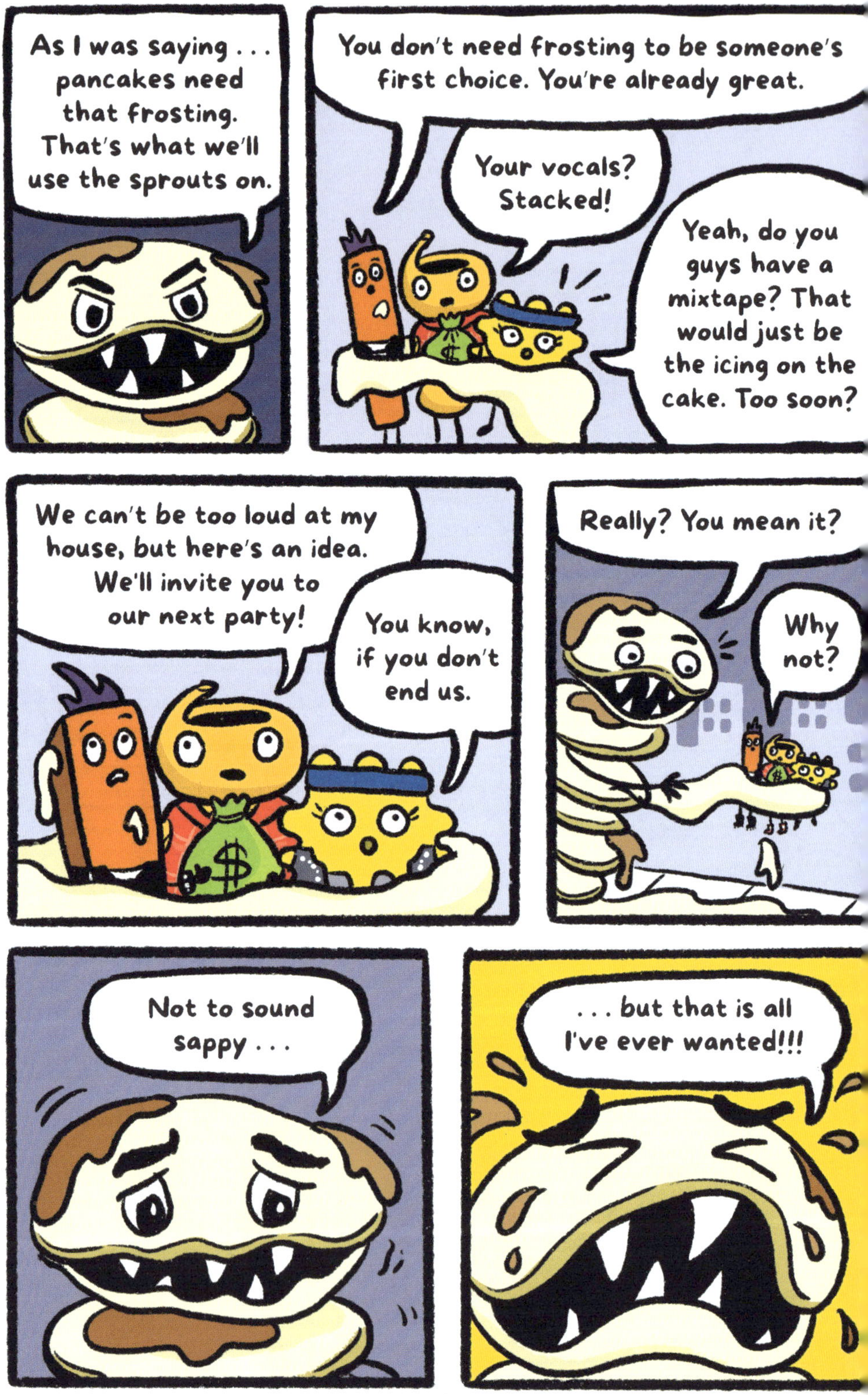
As I was saying . . . pancakes need that frosting. That's what we'll use the sprouts on.
You don't need frosting to be someone's first choice. You're already great.
Your vocals? Stacked!
Yeah, do you guys have a mixtape? That would just be the icing on the cake. Too soon?
We can't be too loud at my house, but here's an idea. We'll invite you to our next party!
You know, if you don't end us.
Really? You mean it?
Why not?
Not to sound sappy . . .
. . . but that is all I've ever wanted!!!

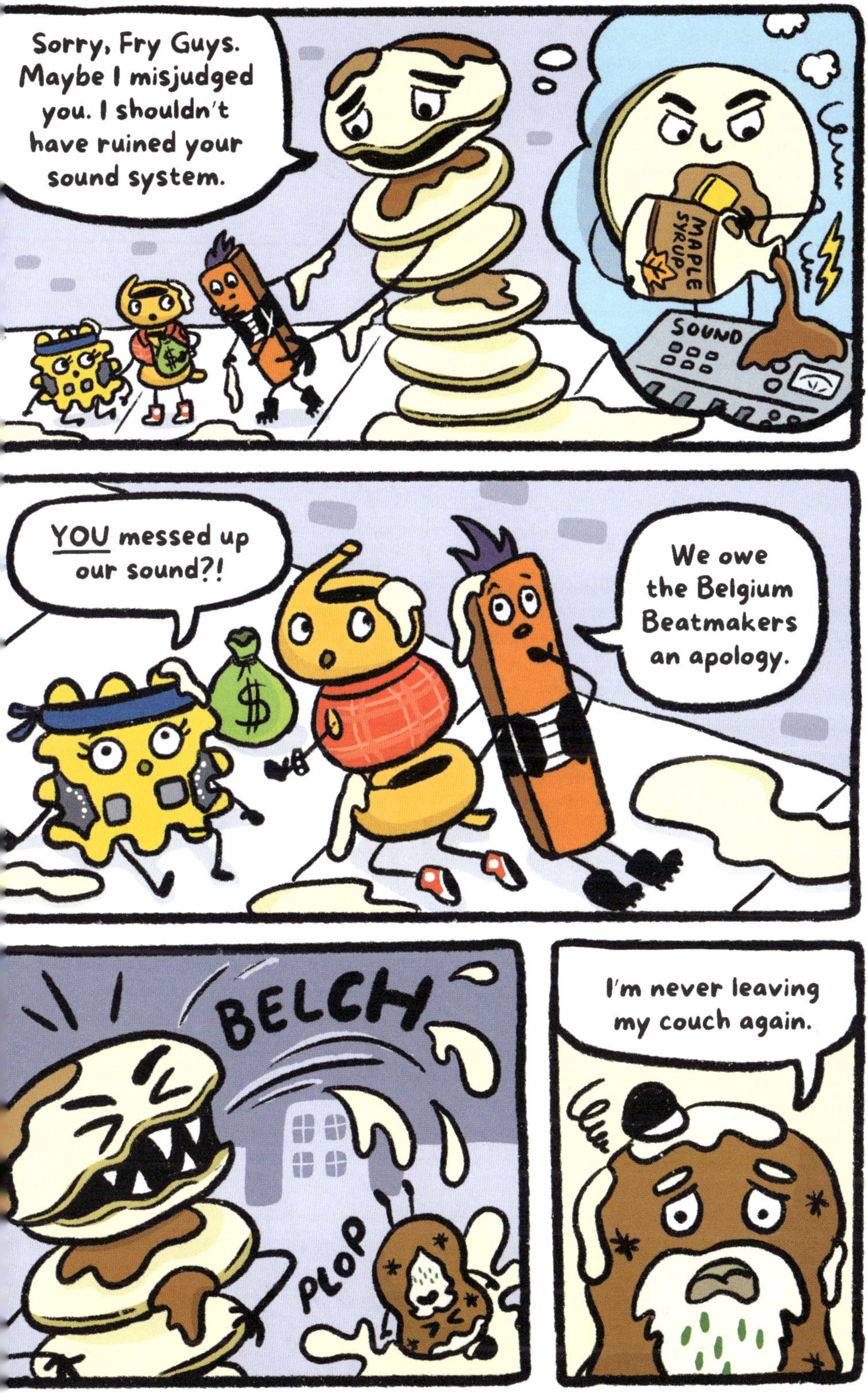
Sorry, Fry Guys. Maybe I misjudged you. I shouldn't have ruined your sound system.
MAPLE SYRUP
SOUND
YOU messed up our sound?!
We owe the Belgium Beatmakers an apology.
BELCH
PLOP
I'm never leaving my couch again.

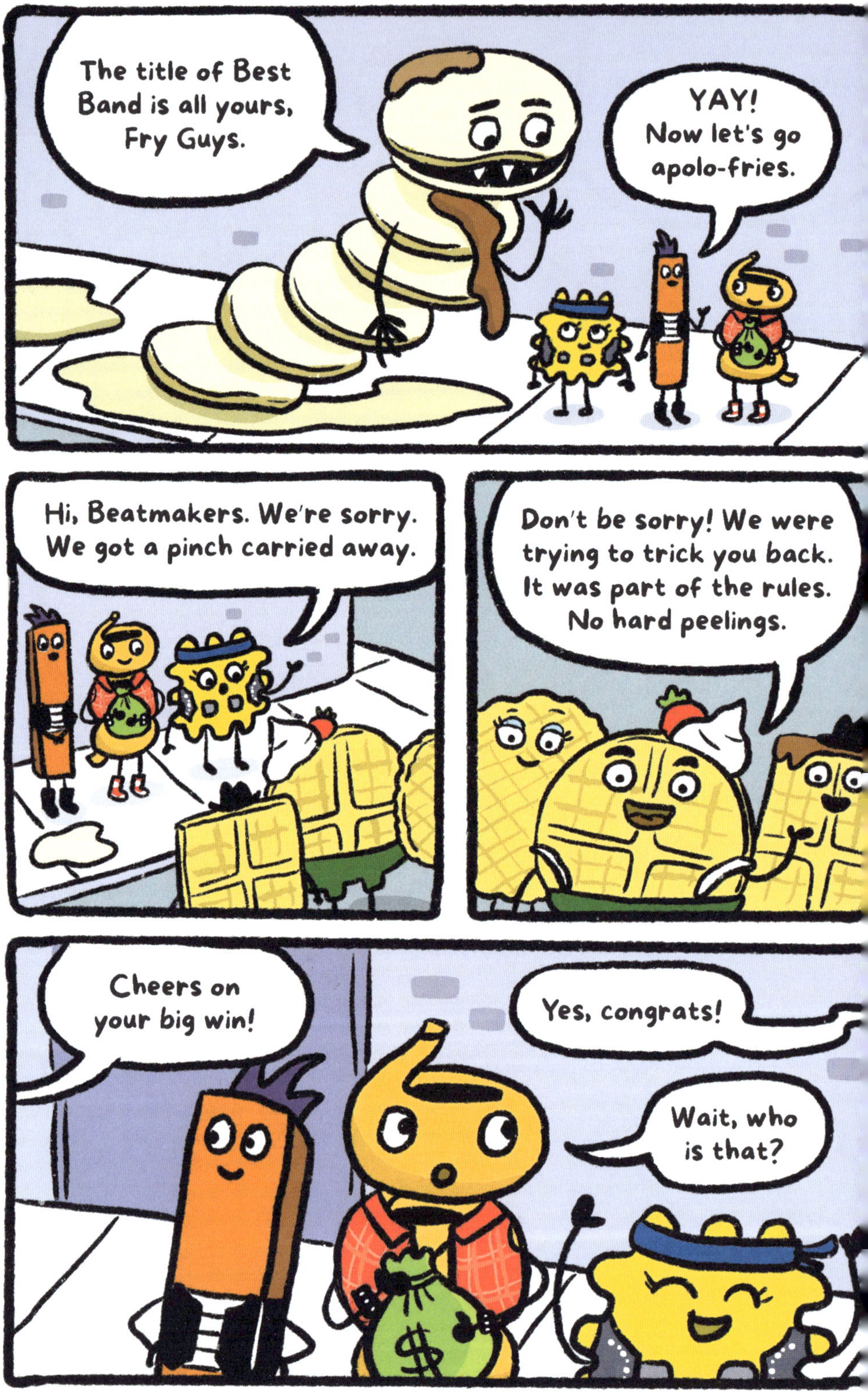
The title of Best Band is all yours, Fry Guys.
YAY! Now let's go apolo-fries.
Hi, Beatmakers. We're sorry. We got a pinch carried away.
Don't be sorry! We were trying to trick you back. It was part of the rules. No hard peelings.
Cheers on your big win!
Yes, congrats!
Wait, who is that?

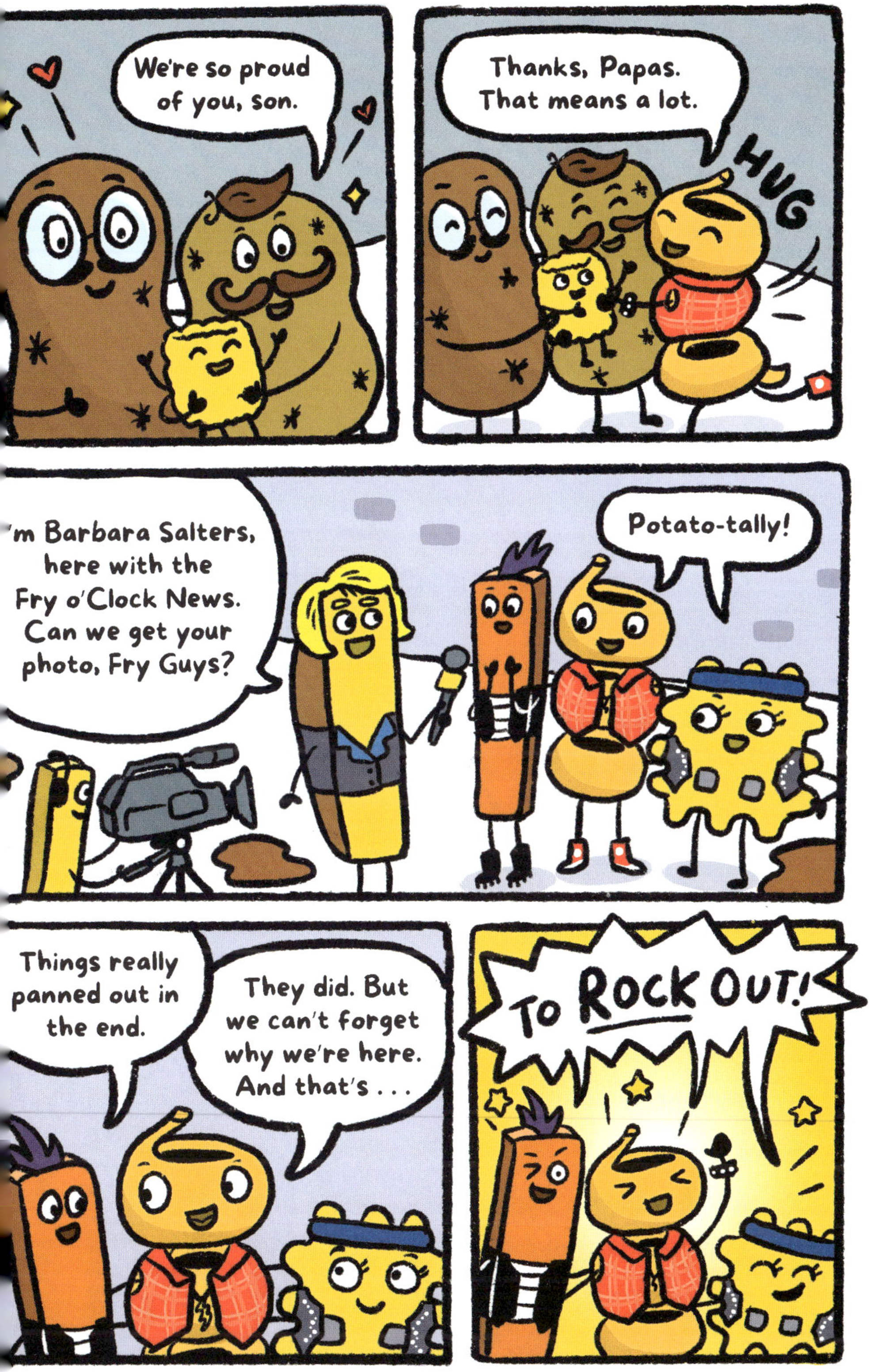
We're so proud of you, son.
Thanks, Papas. That means a lot.
HUG
'm Barbara Salters, here with the Fry o'Clock News. Can we get your photo, Fry Guys?
Potato-tally!
Things really panned out in the end.
They did. But we can't forget why we're here. And that's . . .
TO ROCK OUT!

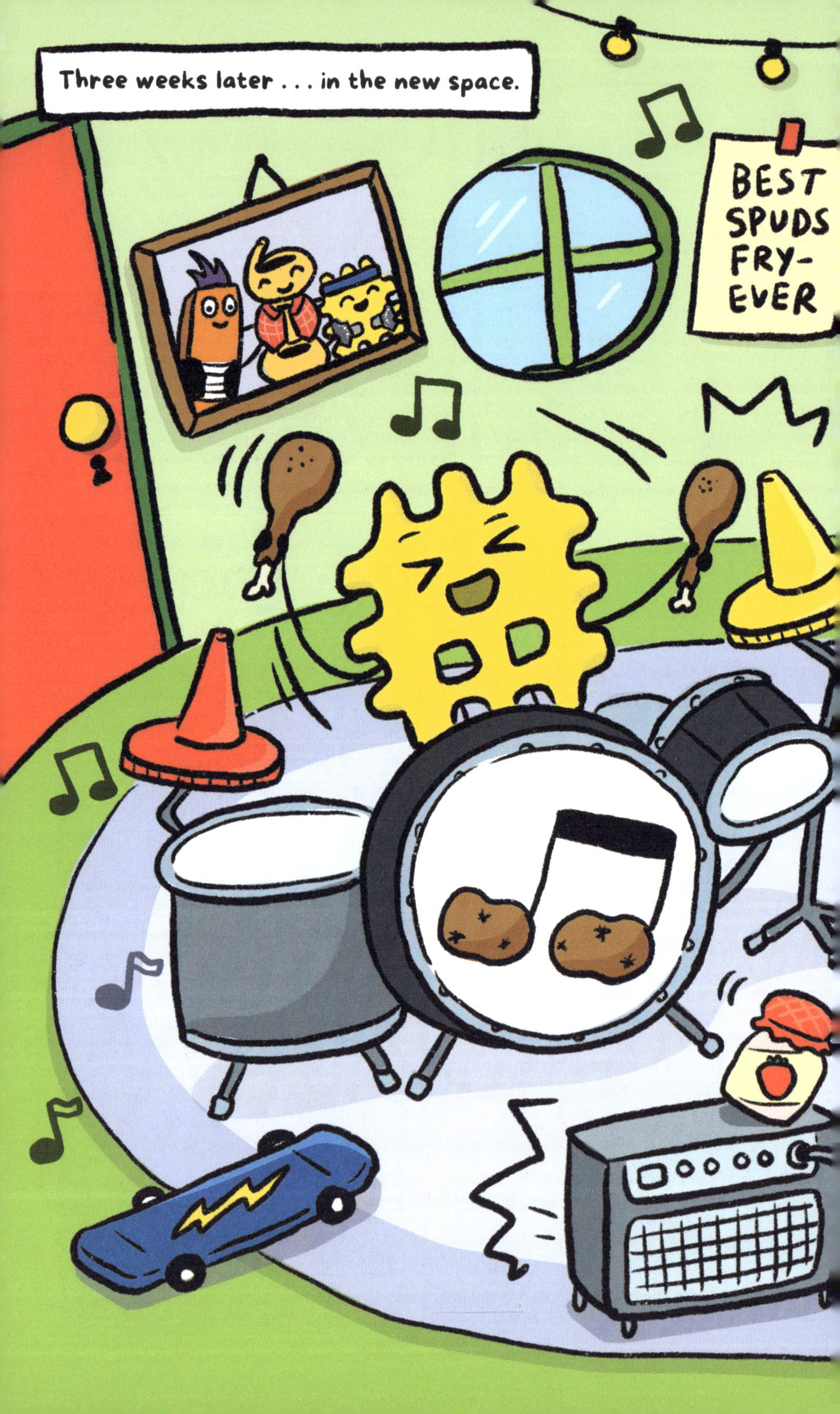
Three weeks later . . . in the new space.
BEST SPUDS FRY-EVER